The Newspaper
Kids 2

NEWSPAPER
OFFICE

Mandy Miami and the Miracle Motel

Juanita Phillips

Illustrations by Mark David

Collins

An Imprint of HarperCollins*Publishers*

*For Dugald — who took my hand and showed me
the way back to the playground ~ J. P.*

First published in Australia by **Angus&Robertson** in 1996
An imprint of HarperCollins*Publishers*, Australia
First published in Great Britain by Collins 1999
Collins is an imprint of HarperCollins*Publishers* Ltd,
77-85 Fulham Palace Road, Hammersmith, London W6 8JB

The HarperCollins website address is www.**fire**and**water**.com

3 5 7 9 8 6 4 2

Text copyright © Juanita Phillips 1996

ISBN 0 00 675461 9

The author asserts the moral right to be identified as author of the work

Printed and bound in Great Britain by
Omnia Books Limited, Glasgow

Chapter One

Something was tickling my nose. I woke up and opened one eye. Pitch black. I couldn't see a thing. Then I remembered what day it was and sat bolt upright in bed.

Christmas morning!

Whatever it was that had been tickling my nose was now hanging in my face. I swatted it out of the way like a fly and turned on my bedside light to see what it was — a piece of mosquito net, ragged around the edges, hanging from a string attached to a hook in the ceiling.

I blinked a couple of times to make sure I wasn't still dreaming. Nope, it was there all right. A piece of mosquito net. My eye followed the string. It went up to the hook, then out through the door that connected my room with Jasper's.

I was old enough to know it wasn't Santa Claus who'd put it there. Sure enough, there was a note attached to it, written in the same big curly handwriting that signed our report cards; Mum's.

'*Merry Christmas, Hugo!*' it said. '*Go and wake your sister.*'

I followed the string into Jasper's room and shook the long skinny lump underneath the duvet. It didn't move. Jasper slept on her stomach, face down with her arms flung out to the side. She looked like a lizard that had been run over by a truck. Anyone else would have died of suffocation, but not old Jasper. Her mouth was too big. She could suck in air from anything, even a pillow.

I lifted a big clump of orange hair out of the way and yelled right in her ear, 'Get up! It's Christmas!'

That got her moving. 'Why didn't you tell me?' she said crossly, snapping awake without even a stretch or a yawn. Even her freckles looked cross.

'I just did.'

'What's the time?'

'I don't know. Early. It's still dark.'

'Come on then, let's open our presents.' Jasper's eleven — one year older than me — and she likes to be in charge. She flicked on her bedside light and rolled out of bed. 'Hey, what's this?' She touched the string. It was stretched tightly around her bedpost, leading out into the hallway.

'Oh, look, Hugo, there's a note.' She squinted at it in the dim light. 'It says, *Follow me*.'

'As if we wouldn't,' I sighed. 'Mum and Dad are so obvious. I just hope it's not as complicated as last year's treasure hunt.'

Sometimes I wished our parents would be normal for once and put all our presents under the Christmas tree like everyone else. But they got such a kick out of hiding the best ones that Christmas got weirder and weirder every year. Last year, they'd sent us on two separate treasure hunts. Jasper found one skate in the washing machine, and I found another up a tree. Luckily, they matched.

'Christmas is really for parents,' I told her. 'We have to humour them. Otherwise they'd be disappointed.'

Jasper frowned. 'I don't get it.' She held up something I hadn't noticed before. 'It's a hair net, an old-fashioned one like Great-aunt Miranda uses. It looks like the one she wraps around her bun to stop it falling off her head. It was attached to the note.'

I touched it. It felt soft and stretchy.

'You got a hair net, I got a piece of mosquito net,' I shrugged. 'Who knows what it means?'

'Well, it must mean something.'

I grabbed Jasper and started following the string out the door.

'It means we've got warped parents,' I said. 'Come on. Let's go and collect the loot.'

'This must be the longest piece of string in the universe,' I grumbled. We were trudging through knee-deep grass in the backyard, and still the string went on. 'Look! It goes over the fence. They must have hidden something in the Stacketts' backyard.'

Jasper didn't answer. She was like a bloodhound on the scent of a murderer.

'Hey, Jasper!' I knew this would get her attention. 'I had a look under the Christmas tree on the way out. I think I saw something . . .'

'Really?' Jasper stopped so suddenly I banged right into the back of her. 'What shape? Skate shape? Book shape?' She was grilling me like a sergeant major. 'Don't tell me it was doll shape or I'll scream . . .'

'No, there were no doll shapes,' I assured her. 'Looked like a CD shape.'

'Mmmm . . . a CD would be great,' mused Jasper, setting off across the Stacketts' backyard again. 'As long as it's not that stupid Mandy Miami you like.'

'Mandy's brilliant!' I said indignantly.

'She's a dill.'

'She is not!'

'Look,' said Jasper, 'anyone who dances around wearing T-shirts that don't cover their bellybutton has to be short of a few brain cells.'

'Oh, right, and I suppose you think Razor X and the Paper Cuts are really smart,' I retorted angrily. 'I suppose when they get sick of breaking guitars over their own heads they'll become nuclear scientists.'

'Razor X is a good musician *and* she makes statements.'

'She makes a mess,' I muttered. 'At least Mandy makes people feel happy. '

'Come on, stop lagging! Looks like this string is going all the way to Toby's.' Jasper gestured furiously at me to catch up. I was so mad that I'd almost forgotten what we were doing out here.

The string continued through a hole in the Stacketts' fence, over into our friend Toby's yard. From there, it stretched up through the fork of the big gum tree, way over our heads, and up into the second-floor window of Toby's bedroom. Then it disappeared.

'What on earth . . .' Jasper turned to me. 'What do we do now?'

I pointed at something white fluttering in the early morning breeze. 'Look. Another note.'

'*Pull this string and wait*,' read Jasper out loud. She tugged at the string. From Toby's bedroom we heard the faint sound of a bell tinkling.

'This must have taken our parents all night to set up,' I said admiringly. 'That's why Mr Trotter came over so late! We should have guessed something was up.'

'Well, whatever it is, I wish they'd just wrapped it up and put it under the tree,' complained Jasper. 'Looks like we've got to split it three ways, too. I know Toby's my best friend, but it's bad enough having to share presents with you . . .'

Just then, we heard the back door open. It was Toby, dressed in a pair of red cotton pyjamas with Christmas trees all over them. He squinted through his thick spectacles and waved when he saw it was us.

'Thanks for the wake-up call,' he said. 'What's the story?'

Toby's the editor of our newspaper, *Street Wise*. That's what he says whenever he wants to know what's happening. Jasper and I are the reporters, so we're supposed to know.

Jasper and I looked at each other and shrugged.

'Search me. We had to follow the string here and we have,' I explained. 'We're looking for our Christmas present. I guess this means you've got something to do with it.'

'Well, this must be a clue.' Toby held up something he was carrying in his right hand.

It was a piece of fishing net. There were even a couple of small lead weights still attached to it. I knew what it was because our Uncle Pete had one at his beach shack on the north coast.

'I woke up when I heard the bell, and this was hanging in my face.' He held the net up. 'There was also a note, saying to go to the Cave. Any idea what this is all about?'

'Well, I got a hair net and Hugo got a bit of mosquito net.' Jasper shook her head, bewildered. 'Now you've got a fishing net. Don't ask me what it all means. Maybe the answer's in the Cave. Come on.'

We traipsed along behind her to the Cave which was an old wooden shed we used as our newspaper office. Only six months ago, it had been our hideaway, our secret meeting place. Now every kid in Blue Rock knew this was the place to come when they had a story worth telling. It wasn't just the sign over the door saying 'Newspaper Office'. Inside, the Cave was a real live newsroom. There were copies of the first three issues of *Street Wise* strewn all over the place. At one end of the Cave, there was the story list — a big sheet of butcher's paper with a list of the stories we were working on. And, of course, there was Myron — Toby's computer.

Everything we wrote went into Myron and came out via the printer as an eight-page newspaper. First, the stories went in. Then Toby wrote headlines in big letters to go over the top. The last things to go in were the photographs, which my best friend Frankie took. Toby always left a hole for pictures so he could drop them in at the last minute. He just scanned the photographs into Myron and trimmed them to the right shape using his computer cursor. Easy! Toby said it was like putting together a big jigsaw puzzle.

But thanks to Christmas, the jigsaw had been lying there untouched for a couple of weeks. Right now, the only thing we newspaper kids had to figure out was what all these clues meant.

'What did you get your dad for Christmas, Toby?' I asked while he fiddled with the combination lock to the Cave.

'If I had a magic wand I would have got him a girlfriend,' sighed Toby. 'But I don't, so I got him socks instead.'

He opened the door and we stepped inside.

'That's what the note said. *Go to the Cave.* So we're here. Now what?' he asked.

The three of us looked around.

'Looks just the same to me,' I said, doing a quick check for wrapping paper. 'If they've left any Christmas presents in here, they must have buried them underground. Maybe we should start digging.'

Behind his thick spectacles, Toby blinked rapidly. That meant his brain was working even harder than normal. 'There *must* be something different.

Another clue. There has to be a good reason they brought the three of us together in the Cave on Christmas morning . . .'

It was Jasper who noticed it.

'Hey! Look at Myron!'

Trust old eagle-eyes. She'd spotted it within two seconds.

I rushed over. 'It's my butterfly net! I was looking for that last week.' Now, it had turned up out of the blue, stretched over the computer terminal as though Myron was a gigantic moth. The whole thing was getting more mysterious by the second. I grabbed the handle of the butterfly net and yanked it free.

The three of us stared at it, completely baffled. Suddenly, a slow grin started to spread over Toby's face. He reached over and turned the computer on.

'What are you doing, Toby? We don't want to play computer games,' said Jasper irritably, as Myron hummed and beeped into action. 'We're looking for our Christmas present.'

Toby started laughing. He had the modem going too.

'This *is* our Christmas present,' he said, typing madly.

Jasper and I looked at him blankly.

'Don't you see? Mosquito net — hair net — fishing net — butterfly net.' Toby was more excited than I'd ever seen him. 'That's our Christmas present — the Net! We're on the Net!'

It took a few seconds for the penny to drop.

Jasper gasped. She grabbed me by the shoulders and shook me.

'The Internet, Hugo!' she yelled. 'We're on the Internet!'

Toby looked up from the computer and nodded. 'Welcome to the World Wide Web!' His grin stretched from ear to ear. 'Watch out everyone ... the newspaper kids are on the Internet!'

We'd just tapped into a computer game library in Brazil when there was a knock on the door.

'That'll be our parents,' said Toby absently, downloading a sample of the new Skeletor game onto Myron. 'I guess they've got to lay down a few rules about the phone bill before they leave us in peace.'

I jumped up to let them in.

'Brilliant treasure trail!' I said as I opened the door. 'We had no idea . . .'

I stopped in the middle of my sentence. Toby and Jasper looked up.

It wasn't our parents.

It was our arch enemy. Lying, cheating, sneaking and lower than a worm's belly.

'Merry Christmas,' said Howard Fitzherbert.

Chapter Two

Inside the Cave, you could have heard a mosquito sneeze.

It was Jasper who finally broke the silence. 'We thought you were still at Sergeant Butch Hardknuckle's Camp for Boys. In the wilderness. Being disciplined.'

'I was. Now I'm not.'

Howard leaned against the doorway. He looked different, somehow. He'd lost some weight, that was one thing. He wasn't as soft and blobby around the edges. But there was something else . . . something I couldn't quite put my finger on.

'So what happened? Did they chuck you out or did you escape?'

That's my sister for you — as subtle as a chainsaw.

'Neither,' Howard replied pleasantly. 'I graduated with honours, just in time for Christmas.'

I couldn't help myself. 'What was it like eating witchetty grubs? Were they all slimy and squishy and revolting?'

Howard stared at me for a long time before answering. 'No — actually they were quite sweet and nutty. The Aborigines consider them a delicacy.'

An uncomfortable silence fell. Finally, Toby voiced the question that was on everybody's mind. 'Howard, what do you want?'

Howard smiled. 'Just paying a visit to my friends. There's no law against that, is there? At least, there wasn't the last time I checked.'

I couldn't say what it was but something worried me. Something about the way Howard was looking at us. It was too . . . nice.

'FRIENDS?' flared Jasper. 'The last time you were here, you infected Myron with a virus and nearly put the newspaper out of business. That's why you were sent to Butch Hardknuckle's Camp, remember? You don't exactly qualify as our friend, Howard.'

'Oh, yes. The newspaper.' Howard's eyes flicked around the Cave. He seemed to be taking it all in. 'It's a big success, I hear.'

'You bet it is!' I boasted. 'Circulation's up to eighty-five. That's over three times what we started at. We're even taking paid advertisements now. Ten dollars for a quarter page, a dollar for classifieds. Porky Merron's sister reckons her baby-sitting business has taken off like a rocket since she started advertising with us.'

'Hmmm, very impressive.'

I could see Howard staring hard at our story list, which was pinned up at the other end of the room. At the top of it we'd written 'New Teacher' in big letters. That was one of the stories we were working on. Miss Finch, the grade five teacher, wasn't coming back after the Christmas holidays. She was going back-packing in Tibet — and we wanted to find out who her replacement was before we went back to school. With any luck we'd get a photograph *and* an interview.

'Hey!' said Jasper. 'Eyes off, Howard!' She'd spotted him, too.

'Howard, I think we've established you're not here for a friendly visit.' Toby sounded edgy. 'So why don't you tell us what you really want and leave us alone?'

Howard nodded. 'Fair enough. I know when I'm not welcome. I just wanted to apologise.'

My mouth fell open so far my jaw hit the ground. *Crunch!* Well, almost.

'APOLOGISE?' asked Jasper and Toby at exactly the same time. They looked as astonished as I was.

'Yes, apologise,' said Howard mildly. 'I know what I did was wrong, and I'm sorry.'

It sounded too good to be true. Howard Fitzherbert, rat extraordinaire . . . apologising?

'Boy. You've changed,' I said suspiciously. 'What happened at Butch Hardknuckle's? Did the witchetty grubs affect your brain?'

Howard chuckled. 'No, Hugo, I simply learned that there's a right and a wrong way to do things. Putting the virus in your computer was the wrong way.'

'Well, I'm glad you've turned over a new leaf.' It sounded good to me. 'Apology accepted, Howard.'

'Hang on, Hugo.' Toby held up his hand to silence me. 'Not so fast.'

He turned to Howard. 'You said that putting the virus in the computer was the wrong way. The wrong way to do what? Destroy us?'

'Exactly, Trotter,' replied Howard. His pale eyes glittered.

'And I assume you think there's a right way?' continued Toby quietly.

'Correct,' answered Howard politely.

'And what would that be?' Toby hadn't taken his eyes off Howard. In fact, the two of them were eyeballing each other so hard that Jasper and I might as well have been on another planet.

Howard didn't answer straightaway. He bent down,

picked a blade of grass, and started chewing it. 'You know, I learned something very interesting out in the wilderness,' he said thoughtfully, 'thanks to you three.' His eyes flicked from me to Jasper and came to rest again on Toby. 'It's called the survival of the fittest. Have you heard of it?'

'Of course.' Toby shrugged. 'Also known as the law of the jungle. The stronger animals survive, the weaker ones don't.'

Howard nodded. 'That's what Butch taught us out in the bush.'

I was losing track. 'What's that got to do with us?'

'Everything.' Howard spat the grass out. Suddenly, the look in his eyes hardened. 'The law of the jungle applies to business as well. The strong businesses survive, the weak go under.'

'Get to the point, Howard,' said Toby evenly.

'The point is that people only buy your newspaper because there isn't anything better.' Howard gave a triumphant smile. 'At least, there *wasn't* anything better. But that's all about to change.'

'You wouldn't,' breathed Jasper. 'You wouldn't dare . . .'

'Oh, yes, I would, Jasper,' replied Howard mockingly. I could see now that his politeness had all been a big act. 'Sorry to be the one to tell you, but as of now, you've got competition. Me.'

The three of us stared at him in stunned silence.

'I'm starting up my own newspaper,' announced Howard Fitzherbert. 'And it'll be so good that nobody will even think about buying yours.'

He turned on his heel and started to walk away. Then he stopped.

'In fact, I guarantee you that after one issue of *my* paper, *Street Wise* will be out of business.' He flashed us an evil smile. 'Merry Christmas.'

'Do you think he means it?' I asked. 'Maybe he's just bluffing. He's always been a bully. He's probably just trying to scare us.'

Toby shook his head. He looked worried.

'I think he's deadly serious. Howard wants revenge, and he wants to do it in a way that won't get him into trouble.'

Jasper was pacing the floor of the Cave. 'It makes perfect sense, when you think about it. What better way to get at us than attack our newspaper?' She slumped into one of the old couches and put her head in her hands. 'He's probably been planning it the whole time he was at Butch Hardknuckle's.'

Suddenly it didn't seem like Christmas anymore. All the fun and excitement had gone out of the morning. I'd even forgotten about our Christmas present — the Internet. Just half an hour ago we'd been talking about how we could use it to make the newspaper better. We were even planning a story on it: '*Street Wise* Goes Web Wide' was the headline. But now, thanks to Howard, everything we had worked so hard for was in danger. I could feel all three of us sliding into a big puddle of gloom.

Toby clicked his fingers.

'Snap out of it, Hugo,' he ordered. 'You too, Jasper. You're acting as though *Street Wise* is already finished. Howard's made a threat — nothing more.'

'Yeah, but what if he does start his own newspaper?' Jasper sounded panicky. 'He's got a better computer than us. And his parents give him so much money, he could make a really good newspaper. We never counted on that.'

'So what? He probably will start his own newspaper. But that doesn't mean it'll be better than ours.' Toby picked up the last edition of *Street Wise* and waved it in the air. 'Look at this!'

'CAUGHT IN THE ACT!' screamed the headline. It was a great story — one of our best.

'Remember?' prompted Toby.

Did I ever! Someone had been creeping around people's backyards at night stealing things off their clotheslines. As chief reporter, I'd been given the task of finding out who it was.

It was simple, really. Frankie, our photographer,

and I laid a trap — a warning system of string and empty tin cans. Then we lay in wait.

When the thief stumbled into our booby trap, there was a huge crashing of tin cans. We turned the spotlight on, and Frankie starting shooting pictures. There were people coming from everywhere yelling, 'Stop thief!' and flashbulbs going off all over the place. One day later, there was the thief staring sheepishly at us from the front page of *Street Wise* — Bruce, the Rottweiler from one block away, with Mrs Fletcher's frilly skirt hanging out of his mouth.

'Another mystery solved,' Toby reminded us. 'Remember how happy everyone was to get their clothes back?'

'Bruce had so many stuffed into his kennel he could hardly squeeze into it.' Jasper giggled at the memory. 'He could have opened a clothes shop.'

Just thinking about the story cheered me up.

'That's the sort of story that money can't buy,' continued Toby. 'It takes brains and perseverance. And don't forget, that's just one. We've done heaps.'

I was starting to see what Toby meant. Even with his big flashy computer and lots of money, Howard was going to have a tough time finding stories as good as ours. We had experience now. People in Blue Rock knew us. They liked seeing their photographs on our social page. They thought our

'Doctor Death' silly medical column was funny. They liked what we wrote about and they knew they could trust us to print the truth. That's why they kept buying *Street Wise*.

'Hi, everyone.' It was Frankie. She was the only person except us who was allowed into the Cave without knocking. As usual, she had at least two cameras slung around her neck. 'What's the story? Did you get some good presents?'

We quickly filled her in about Howard and his threat to put us out of business.

'I know,' said Frankie when we finished.

'What!' The three of us stared at her.

'He's already been to see me.' Frankie took the lens cap off one of her cameras, and started pointing it at objects in the Cave. She was practising focussing. 'He offered me a job.' She zoomed in on my face. 'You've got a big wart on your nose, Hugo. With hairs growing out of it.'

'Liar.' I pushed the camera away, laughing uneasily. 'What do you mean, he offered you a job?'

Frankie put the camera down. 'I thought I'd better tell you about it straightaway. It's true — he's going to start up his own newspaper.'

'So he is serious,' Toby said. 'Did he tell you anything?'

'Lots,' said Frankie jubilantly. Her black eyes

danced. 'I let him think I was interested in the job, so he spilled the beans. He's going to call it *Guess What!*'

'Hmm, that's not a bad name.' Toby wrote it down on a piece of paper. 'Anything else?'

'Well, he said he's going to do a medical column called "Doctor Doom".'

'Hey! That's just like ours!' said Jasper angrily. 'It's just a different name.'

'He's going to have a social page, too. And that new teacher — he wants me to help him track down some old students. Interview them. Find out if she's a nightmare.'

Toby stopped scribbling. 'You know, Howard's not as stupid as I thought. He's got some good ideas.'

'But they're our ideas!' I was furious. 'He's just copying!'

Toby sighed. 'That's business, Hugo. Everybody takes ideas from everybody else. The important thing is what you do with them.'

Frankie broke in. 'There is one thing he's doing that's completely different. He says he wants to make a big splash with his first issue. He wants to have a front page story that's so big, everyone will want to read it.'

'Oh yeah?' I was sceptical. 'There's not a lot that

happens in Blue Rock. And if it does, it's in *Street Wise*!'

'He's going to interview a pop star. Someone really famous. He wouldn't tell me who,' said Frankie, 'but his family has lots of connections.'

'It helps us to know that. Good work, Frankie,' nodded Toby. 'I hope you told him you'd take the job?'

'Of course.'

I looked at her, dumbfounded. Frankie's my best friend and I couldn't believe what I was hearing. 'But you work for us!'

Frankie grinned. 'Ever heard of a double agent, Hugo?'

It suddenly clicked.

This wasn't just a game anymore. It wasn't even just business.

It was war.

Chapter Three

'Turn that music down!'

Two weeks after Christmas and things were pretty much back to normal around our house. Mum was reading the morning paper, and we all had to tippy-toe around the house like someone had died. You'd think she was studying for a big exam, the way she read that paper. She was like a horse feeding out of a nose-bag.

'That's a terrible noise,' she complained, coming up for air. 'Is it someone singing or are they having their toe-nails pulled out one by one?'

'Oh, Mum.' Jasper rolled her eyes. 'It's Razor X, singing a very important song about the crew-cut Pygmies in Peru. She's standing up for their rights.'

'What's all that banging?'

'It's her band, Mum, the Paper Cuts. They're smashing their guitars to express their anger at the Pygmies' trees being cut down. It's a protest song.'

'Well, it sounds horrible. Take it off.'

Dad poured her another cup of tea. 'You've only got yourself to blame, Jennifer,' he said, amused. 'You gave it to her for Christmas.'

'I hate it.' Mum buried her head in the *Blue Rock Bugle*. 'Why don't we put on that other one? Hugo's favourite. That girl who sings the love songs.'

'Gag.' Jasper put her forefinger in her mouth and pretended to throw up. 'The Singing Navel. Mandy Miami, how uncool. She never stands up for anyone's rights. In fact, she doesn't even have opinions about anything! She just sings sappy, pappy love songs.'

'That's not true!' I said.

Jasper and I had had this argument before but nothing seemed to change her mind.

'It is true! When have you ever heard Mandy Miami talk about anything important?' Jasper looked at me triumphantly. 'Never! Because she never talks about anything at all!'

She was right about that. Mandy Miami was one of the world's most famous pop stars, but she was also one of the most reclusive. Unlike Razor X, who was always appearing on television music shows, Mandy kept to herself. Nobody knew much about her. Her record company said she was shy, that's why she didn't give interviews. She had millions of fans but none of us knew anything about her — only the snippets that popped up occasionally in music magazines. I knew she'd been discovered on a talent show in Australia and now she lived in Los Angeles, making records. I knew she was about to visit Blue Rock as part of her Australian concert tour. But that was it.

'The local girl made good,' said Dad.

Razor X's strangulated scream was cut off in mid-howl as I pressed the stop button and slipped a Mandy Miami CD into the player.

'Well, good luck to her. And you never know, Jasper — one day, she might give an interview and you'll discover she's not so bad after all,' Dad laughed.

Jasper pulled a face. 'THAT would take a miracle.' She stuck her fingers in her ears and stalked off. 'I'm going to surf the Net.'

'Remember the rules,' Dad called out. 'Don't forget there's a time limit on that thing. We're not millionaires . . .'

The back door banged shut. I watched thoughtfully as Jasper stomped off in the direction of the Cave.

Something that Dad had said had given me an idea . . .

'You've got to be kidding!' Jasper screeched. 'An interview with Mandy Miami? You must be nuts, Hugo.'

We were sitting in the Cave having another crisis meeting about the newspaper. Since Howard's visit two weeks ago, we hadn't seen him. But we'd heard plenty. According to our spy, he wasn't wasting any time stealing our ideas and our customers. The rat! Already we'd had three kids cancel their classified ads and ask for their money back. Porky Merron's sister was one of them. 'Nothing personal,' she apologised, pocketing her two dollar refund. 'But Howard's just rung me on his new mobile phone. He says he'll run my ad for free if I switch to his newspaper.'

'Well, we have to do something.' Toby looked grim. 'Quite frankly, I'm open to all ideas. This issue is just about ready to print but we still don't have a lead story. And whatever it is, it has to be better than *Guess What*'s front page.'

'That's my point,' I said. 'We already know Howard wants to interview a pop star. So let's make sure that our pop star is bigger and better than his.'

'But Mandy Miami's music stinks,' argued Jasper. 'If we're going to interview a pop star, why not Razor X? At least we know she'll talk to us.'

'That's the problem,' said Toby. 'Razor X talks to *everyone*. The whole world knows what she thinks. The point of an exclusive interview is that nobody else has it.

'I think it's a great idea,' said Frankie stoutly. 'Mandy will make a good front page photo, too.'

I smiled at her gratefully.

'Three against one, I guess you win.' Jasper looked miffed. 'But you still haven't explained how we're going to get the interview in the first place. Every paper in the world has been chasing her for years. And she lives in Los Angeles, for heaven's sake.'

'Most of the time,' I corrected her. 'But she also tours the world. And as it happens, she's coming to Australia next week.' I waved a magazine clipping at her.

The way I looked at it, *Street Wise* had as much chance as anybody else of getting an interview with Mandy Miami. True, we didn't have a clue where to start — but then neither did anyone else. Even the big music magazines were baffled by her. They called her 'Mystery Mandy'. One magazine even offered a reward of one thousand dollars to anyone who could track her down when she was on tour. But nobody ever won it. Mandy arrived at her concerts in a big black limousine, sang for two hours, and then disappeared. One time, the members of her fan club took it in turns to ride the elevators of every flash hotel in town, twenty-four hours a day, just to see if they could catch her. But she wasn't at any of them — or if she was, she used the stairs. Yep, Mandy was a mystery all right. It was like she vanished into thin air.

We had one big thing in our favour — my background as a reporter, which was a bit like being a detective. Mandy Miami wasn't a criminal, of course — but tracking her down was the same sort of thing. I knew from experience that no matter how hard somebody tried, they always left at least one clue behind them. It was my job to find it.

Toby looked at me thoughtfully. 'Usually I'd say it was an impossible story, Hugo. The international aspect would normally make it too difficult for a small paper like ours.' He patted the computer monitor. 'But thanks to Santa Claus, the world is a much smaller place these days.'

Of course — the Internet! Toby had given us a couple of lessons and already we were experts. It was funny to think that millions of people all over the world were sitting at their computers — just like we were — and we could talk to all of them! From our little newspaper office in Blue Rock, Australia, we could reach out and touch almost every corner of the planet. And somewhere in that gigantic, world-wide web of information was something — or someone —

that would lead me to Mandy Miami. I could feel it in my bones.

'Let's do it!' Toby made his decision. He walked to the story list and picked up the thick black felt pen.

Frankie nudged me jubilantly. We watched as Toby wrote in big black letters on the story list: 'Project X'.

'We'll give it a code name,' he explained. 'That way, if Howard or any of his spies come snooping, they won't know what we're doing.' He turned to Jasper. 'How are you going with the new teacher? Just in case Hugo can't find Mandy Miami, Miss Finch's replacement becomes our lead story. It's our back-up.'

Jasper snapped to attention. 'One step ahead of you, boss.' She flicked her plaits in a very businesslike way. 'I'm hoping to have a name for you tomorrow.'

She'd obviously come up with a plan. Hopefully, it would work so we could get to the new teacher before Howard did. From the information Frankie was able to get to us, he hadn't tracked her down either. Mind you, I had no intention of letting Jasper snaffle the front page. That was mine — and Mandy's.

'Good,' said Toby. 'We need the name before we can do anything else. And we need it before Howard gets it.'

Before we could get any further, there was a knock on the door. It was Mr Trotter, Toby's dad.

'Hi kids! How's the paper going? Getting lots of scoops?'

'You bet, Mr Trotter!' I liked Toby's dad. He was a reporter on the local paper, so he understood the business. He wasn't too strict, either. He was a lot younger than most parents and he never seemed to mind how late Toby stayed up. In fact, he was more like an untidy big brother than a father. He was always trying to sneak out of the house in a crumpled shirt and a tie with tomato sauce dribbles on it — but Toby always caught him and made him change. Toby made sure he ate properly and got out of bed in the morning. Sometimes he had to tip a glass of cold water on him to do it but, thanks to Toby, Mr Trotter hadn't been late for work for six months.

'Anything wrong, Dad?' I could tell Toby was worried about him. 'How come you're not at work?'

'Lunch break. A man's got to eat!' He winked at me. 'Can't catch those criminals on an empty stomach, hey, Hugo?'

He turned to Toby. 'Actually, I've had another call from the welfare people.'

'Another one!' Toby groaned. 'What do they want this time?'

Mr Trotter waved his hand dismissively. 'Oh, the same old thing. They think I'm neglecting you, leaving you to run wild on the streets while I'm at work.'

'It's all those cars you've been stealing,' joked Jasper. 'You've really got to stop it, Toby.'

Mr Trotter looked at him anxiously.

'You're all right here on your own, aren't you, son? I can try to take some time off work if you like.'

Toby shook his head. 'No way, Dad. You'd only get under our feet. We're too busy at the moment working on the next issue of *Street Wise*.'

'Ah.' Mr Trotter nodded knowingly. 'Deadlines. I understand.' He looked relieved. 'I'll leave you to it.'

After he left, Toby thumped his fist on the desk. 'Those rotten welfare people! I wish they'd leave Dad in peace.' He sighed.

'Maybe your dad will get married again!' suggested Jasper. Her eyes lit up. 'That's what we need — a matchmaker! Someone to find him a girlfriend!'

Toby looked at her doubtfully.

'In the olden days, marriages were always arranged by a village matchmaker,' Jasper continued. 'I read about it in a book. They had a lot of power. Even kings and queens went to them for help.' She flicked her plaits. 'I would have been great at it.'

'You just like the idea of bossing a king around,' I said, to stir her up. 'You'd be there at the wedding altar, answering all the questions for him. Yes, he will. Yes, of course he does.'

Jasper looked huffy. 'Rubbish. I'm just a good organiser.'

'Forget it, Jasper,' said Toby. 'You can't organise people to fall in love.'

Jasper raised an eyebrow. 'You'd be surprised,' she said archly. 'You'd be surprised what I can organise.'

After the meeting, we took the short cut home through the Stacketts' backyard.

'What was all that about?' I asked Jasper.

She smiled smugly. 'I just thought I'd kill two birds with one stone.'

'What?' Jasper was talking gibberish again.

'Finding Miss Finch's replacement *and* finding a girlfriend for Mr Trotter.' She looked meaningfully at me. 'Two birds, Hugo.'

'Huh?' My mind was on other things. Like finding Mandy Miami.

Jasper rolled her eyes. 'Never mind, Hugo.'

She stomped off impatiently, muttering to herself. 'Boys!' I heard her say as she squeezed through the fence.

Chapter Four

I looked at the clock. 2.30 am. Outside, it was pitch black and stormy, the wind whistling through the gum trees. Everybody else in Blue Rock was fast asleep. I shivered, half-scared and half-excited. If Mum or Dad woke up and found me missing, I'd be in big trouble.

'Dear Mandy,' I wrote. 'Allow me to introduce myself. My name is Hugo Lilley. I live in Australia and I'm ten years old. I am a big fan of yours but this is not the reason I'm writing to you. My purpose is "strictly business".'

I sat back from Myron and checked what I'd written. It sounded pretty impressive, I thought —

especially the last bit. I clicked on 'strictly business' and turned it into big purple capitals. Then I underlined it. Then I changed the colour to green and black stripes. There. That should get her attention.

'I am a professional reporter for a newspaper called *Street Wise*,' I continued. I clicked on 'professional' and made it flash on and off in big pink letters. Maybe I was exaggerating just a teeny-weeny bit but what did I have to lose? 'My sister Jasper and my friends, Toby and Frankie, also work for *Street Wise*. It's a really good newspaper, and it's all for kids. Except now a lot of grown-ups buy it too, just to see what we're up to!'

I stopped. Should I tell Mandy the whole sorry saga about Howard? Or should I just ask her for an interview? Really casually, as if we interviewed pop stars every day, and she was really lucky we'd chosen her.

I thought hard. Mandy was a girl and girls always liked to know the gory details. Take my sister. You could never just say, 'Oh, I went to the shop today.' Not to Jasper. She'd throw you up against the nearest wall and demand to know everything. 'Who did you see there? What were they wearing? What did you buy? GIVE ME THE GORY DETAILS!' You were lucky to get out alive unless you answered everything, right down to what colour undies you had on. Mum was the same. She liked to know 'the full story', she said. That's why she bought all those magazines with famous people on the cover and headlines saying, TRAGIC SOAPIE STAR TELLS: MY BRAIN IS MISSING!

Yep, girls liked the full story.

I started writing again. 'But something terrible has happened. A big bully called Howard is trying to run us out of business. So he's started up his own newspaper in competition and, if we don't get a really big story, nobody will want to buy *Street Wise*. That's why I'm writing to you, Mandy. If we have an interview with you, everyone will want to buy *Street Wise*, and Howard will have to find someone else to pick on! So please, please help us. You can E-mail your reply to me at hugo@streetwise.com.au. Signed, your fan, Hugo.'

I re-read the whole thing, then added a PS; 'I don't want to put pressure on you, Mandy, but our lives are in your hands.' Just so she'd know I was joking, I added a smiley :-) like that to the end of it, the way Toby had shown us. I just hoped Mandy knew you had to look at smileys sideways to see what they meant.

With any luck, I'd get a reply straightaway. Sending a letter on the Internet wasn't like sending it the old way, with a piece of paper and an envelope and a stamp. That took a million years, especially if it was going overseas. When you sent a letter on the Internet, it was called E-mail, and it got there in a couple of seconds. You wrote it on a computer, zapped it off and BINGO! There it was on the other person's computer.

A gust of wind rattled the windowpane. I jumped. It wasn't my idea to come to the Cave in the dead of night all on my own — it was Jasper's.

'You know that Los Angeles is a day behind,' Miss Know-it-all told me the night before. 'Fourteen hours to be precise. If you're going to talk to anyone there, you'll have to do it at a time when they're likely to be sitting at their computers.'

'What do you mean, a day behind?' It sounded like science fiction to me.

'Ask Toby, if you don't believe me,' retorted Jasper. 'America is on the other side of the world, right? The sun gets to us before it reaches them, right? So it might be Tuesday morning over here, but it's still the day before — Monday — over there.'

I still didn't get it.

'So if I robbed a bank here on Tuesday morning, I could hop on a plane with all that money, and when I arrived in Los Angeles it would still be Monday?'

'I suppose so.' Jasper shrugged. 'So what?'

'So if it's still Monday, then I haven't committed a crime,' I said triumphantly. 'I'd have the money, without committing a crime.'

'Yes, you did,' argued Jasper. 'You robbed a bank, Hugo.'

'But I robbed it on Tuesday,' I said triumphantly. 'If I turn the clock back to Monday, it hasn't happened. Because it's still the day before.'

It was all very confusing. Not that I wanted to rob a bank. But if I wanted to find Mandy Miami, I had to go to where the trail started. America. And the best time to talk to people was daytime — their daytime. If Jasper was right, 2.30 in the morning our time was about lunchtime over there. It gave me a whole afternoon of American time to track Mandy down.

'You'd better not be pulling my leg,' I threatened Jasper as I set the alarm for 2.00 am. 'I'll have your guts for garters if you're doing this as a joke.'

'Do what you like,' sniffed Jasper, flouncing off to bed. 'I'm only trying to help.'

I didn't tell her I was writing a letter to Mandy. For a start, I didn't even know where to send it. And even if I did find her address, why on earth would Mandy Miami bother replying? She got hundreds of requests for interviews and she'd never agreed to one of them. I had a snowball's chance in hell, and I knew it. But it was worth a shot.

The first hurdle was finding out Mandy's address on the Internet. I typed in the key word, MIAMI, and sent the search robots out to find any matching files.

They came back with a ton of information but all of it was useless. I'd forgotten there was a city in America called Miami. It must have been a city full of computer freaks because everyone — from the Miami Design Your Own Pizza Parlour to the Champion Miami Tea-cosy Knitters — was on the Internet.

I had to narrow the target. I typed in MANDY and MIAMI, and sent the search party out again. This time, only one came up — the Mandy Miami Fan Club.

So Mandy's fans had their own site on the World Wide Web. 'Hmmm,' I thought. 'This could be very interesting . . .'

I clicked in.

Suddenly, I was looking at Mandy. There was a full-colour moving image of her on the computer screen — and she was talking to me!

'Welcome to the Mandy Miami Fan Club home page,' she said. 'For the latest information on my concert dates, click . . . here. To see my latest video clip, click . . . here. For the one and only interview I've ever given to a newspaper, click . . . here. For the Bulletin Board and Latest Sightings, click . . . here.'

It looked like Mandy, but something was wrong. The voice, for a start. This Mandy was speaking in an American accent, not Australian. And when I looked closely, I could see the image on the computer was a still photograph. Only the mouth was moving in time with the words.

It wasn't Mandy at all! Somebody who was very clever with computers had made it look like Mandy was talking.

Still, it was a start.

I waited until the fake Mandy went through her routine again, then clicked into the Bulletin Board. Toby had told us about Bulletin Boards. There were thousands of them on the Web, he said, and they were just like the bulletin board at school. People left messages on them, and you could browse through and read them. Or you could add your own.

There was a section of the bulletin board labelled Fan Mail. 'Leave your messages of love and adoration here and we will forward them on to Mandy at her record company,' it said.

No way, I thought. I didn't want to leave my letter there. Everyone else would be able to read it — and anyway, how did I know that Mandy would even get to see it?

I went back to the main bulletin board and had a look through people's messages, hoping to find one which gave Mandy's personal E-mail address. But it was all silly stuff — a fan in Finland saying he'd spent the last two years making a Mandy Miami statue out of matchsticks. Someone else who collected Mandy stuff, had left a message asking for anything Mandy had ever touched or worn. 'Even a used tea-bag that she has left behind in a cafe,' begged Tran from Korea. Boy, some people were desperate.

Gloomily, I clicked into the Latest Sightings.

> Hey Fanzzz . . . thought you would like to know I saw the mysterious Miss M, hidden behind dark sunglasses, buying groceries at my local supermarket just two days ago. Could be the last sighting before she jets off to Australia for her next big tour! For a full report on what she was wearing and what groceries she bought (pretty amazing folks!), just E-mail Mandy's biggest fan, Papa Razzi. Yeah!

That was the most recent sighting, dated two days ago. Lucky Papa Razzi. He'd got closer to Mandy Miami than I ever would. I couldn't even get a letter to her.

To cheer myself up, I typed in my own Latest Sighting.

> Saw Mandy at the check-out counter of my local K-Mart. She was standing next to Elvis.

I added a sad smiley :-(because that's how I was feeling.

Outside, the wind was blowing so hard the windowpanes in the Cave were rattling. I stared out into the blackness, stumped. What on earth was I doing here instead of being tucked up in my warm bed? I thought the Internet would have all the answers. Instead, I felt like I was wandering through a virtual reality maze full of dead ends and blind alleys. What I really needed was a miracle. I sighed. Even a small one would do.

Suddenly, Myron beeped. My E-mail box was blinking.

I sat up. E-mail? At this hour of the night? Mystified, I moved the mouse and clicked.

> What's wrong with you, smart alec? If you're sad it's probably because you're reporting FAKE SIGHTINGS and there's nothing we REAL FANS hate more. GRRRR!!

It was signed, Papa Razzi.

Chapter Five

Contact! I couldn't believe my luck.

Quickly, I typed a reply.

How do you know it was false? Signed, Smart Alec.

I copped an angry blast in reply.

Because Mandy doesn't shop at K-Mart, that's why. And she's not in Australia yet and that's where your message comes from. Speak the truth Nerd Brain or feel the wrath of those who know the rules! We will bombard your mailbox with angry messages until it BLOWS UP! You have been warned.

Yikes! He was as mad as a nest of hornets. I thought for a minute.

Papa Razzi obviously knew his way around the

Internet. Maybe he could help me — if I calmed him down, that is.

My humblest apologies,

I wrote back.

I'm only new at this! Thanks for the advice.

I waited. Papa Razzi seemed to be deciding whether to ignore me.

Then my mail box beeped again.

Well, if you're a newbie, that explains it,

came the gruff reply.

Just don't do it again! Anyway, how come you're up so late? Isn't it the middle of the night down there?

Yeah. Mum and Dad would kill me if they knew. But I'm on a mission.

I knew that would get him.

What sort of mission?

I'm trying to get an urgent message to Mandy Miami, but I don't know her E-mail address. Maybe you could help me — seeing as you're Mandy's biggest fan.

I held my breath and waited.

Good try, Smart Alec. Mandy's private E-mail address is a well-guarded secret. What have you got to trade for it?

I racked my brains.

> Nothing at the moment. I may have something
> VERY, VERY BIG later on — I can't tell you what
> it is because it's top secret — but I have to get
> my message to Mandy first.

There was a long pause. Papa Razzi
was considering the offer.

> I don't know if I can trust you, Smart Alec, but
> I'm prepared to take a small risk. Here's a clue:
> try her record company.

I stared at the computer screen. Try Mandy's
record company? That wasn't a lot to go on.

I made a final plea to Papa Razzi.

> Then what?

The mail box beeped one more time.

> Figure it out.

I tried again, but there was no reply. He was gone.

'Wake up! Hugo! WAKE UP!'

Someone had stuck superglue in my eyes. I
couldn't open them. I tried, then gave up. 'Go away,'
I groaned.

Two sharp fingers yanked my eyelids open.

'Get up,' ordered Jasper. 'It's nearly lunchtime.
And I've got a name.'

'What . . . ?'

'The new teacher's name! I know what it is.'

'Wheaties, did you say? Mmmm ... I'll have mine with golden syrup please.'

'HUGO!' Jasper pulled the duvet off me. 'Wake up and listen to me. I know who the new teacher is.'

I rubbed the last of the superglue out of my eyes and looked at the clock. 12.20 pm! Why had I slept in so late? Then I remembered — the Internet! The last thing I could remember was sitting in front of Myron and feeling very, very tired ... 'How did I get back home?'

'I dragged you all the way,' Jasper grumbled. 'I'm sure you were sleepwalking. And I've had to tell all sorts of fibs to Mum and Dad so the least you can do is wake up and listen to me.'

I stretched and yawned. 'I'm listening. Give me the gory details.'

'Well.' Jasper plonked herself on my bed and took a deep breath. 'You realise, of course, that the identity of the new teacher is top secret.'

'No kidding.' The four of us — Jasper, Toby, Frankie and I — had just spent the last three weeks since school broke up trying to find out. We'd asked everyone we knew, and nobody had a clue. Even the parents on the P&C committee couldn't tell us anything. The only person who knew was the person who'd hired the new teacher — the school principal, cranky old Miss Weinberger. And nobody was game to ask her.

Jasper lowered her voice. 'In fact, I am one of the few people in the world who knows the name.'

'Well, what is it?' I was getting impatient. 'Who's the new teacher?'

'Ssshhh!' Jasper put her finger to her lips. 'Are you sure this room isn't bugged?'

'The only bug in this room is you, you nit,' I said. 'Come on, spit it out — what's the name?'

Jasper looked huffy. 'I just want you to understand that this is classified information. Highly sensitive.'

'Does that mean you have to kill me after you've told me?'

Jasper ignored the question. 'Strictly speaking, I shouldn't tell anybody until my story is printed. In case the opposition finds out.'

'Okay.' I closed my eyes and rolled over, pretending to go back to sleep. I gave her ten seconds maximum. One, two, three . . .

'Oh, all right. I'll tell you,' Jasper burst out. 'After all, you are my brother. Miss Bishop; first name, Lindsay.'

I opened my eyes. Jasper prodded me gleefully. 'Well? Am I a genius or am I a genius?'

'You're a genius,' I admitted. 'How did you find out?'

She filled me in.

'Remember Miss Finch's farewell party?'

How could anyone forget? It was two days before school broke up. We had to sit at our desks writing boring essays while the teachers went to the staff room for a special tea party. Only problem was, they didn't come back. The noise from the staff room got louder and more raucous. Suddenly the door opened, and our principal, Old Whiney, came charging down the corridor, cackling like a maniac and screaming 'Yee-ha!'. Every so often she'd jump in the air and click her heels together. We all rushed to the windows and watched as Miss Weinberger tap-danced towards the busy road. The other teachers had to chase after her and tackle her to the ground like a footy player to stop her running out into the traffic. While they were doing that, Denis Wong snuck into the staff room to see if there was any food left. But all he found was half a Boston bun, and a silver bucket with a little bit of sherry punch at the bottom of it. Denis reckoned Old Whiney must have drunk the whole bucket.

'Well, I got to thinking,' continued Jasper. 'Miss Weinberger usually doesn't talk to anyone, except to yell at them. Even the teachers. But that day was different. She was a lot more . . . relaxed.'

Relaxed wasn't the word. Old Whiney was using her false teeth as castanets by the time we saw her.

Nuts, bats, completely stark-raving crackers was more like it!

'If ever there was a time when Miss Weinberger was going to let out a secret,' said Jasper, 'it was the day of Miss Finch's farewell. And who do you think she would spend most of her time talking to at the farewell?'

'Miss Finch?' I guessed.

'Exactly! Miss Finch was the star of the show, right? The centre of attention, because she's leaving. The *celebrity*, Hugo.'

Jasper likes celebrities. She wants to be one when she grows up.

'As you know, I've done a lot of research about celebrities.' She meant she read Mum's magazines. 'People are attracted to them and want to be their friends, even if it's just for a short time. And to do that, they often tell them things they wouldn't tell anyone else.'

I looked at Jasper admiringly. She was turning out to be as good a detective as I was!

The next step was easy. Jasper arranged to see Miss Finch to check out her hunch. She said it was because she had a goodbye present for her. Miss Finch was delighted that one of her pupils was being so thoughtful and invited Jasper around for morning tea. That's where she was while I was sleeping.

'Did she say what Miss Bishop is like?'

Jasper frowned, trying to remember.

'I don't think so. All Miss Weinberger said to Miss Finch was that Lindsay Bishop had agreed to take the job. She didn't even say what school she's from.'

Still, it was a good start. As I told Jasper about my own progress on the Internet, I started to feel excited. She had the new teacher's name, and I had made an important contact. It was a little bit like the Christmas treasure hunt — one clue leading to another, and then another. At this rate, Howard Fitzherbert wouldn't see us for dust!

Huh. Was I wrong!

Jasper stuck her nose in the air and sniffed it like a dog.

'Follow the smell!' she said as we headed towards Toby's. 'What do you reckon he's cooking today?'

'Mmmm. Smells delicious. Maybe Thai chicken curry with saffron rice.'

'Nope. It's definitely Italian,' decided Jasper. 'Spaghetti bolognaise. Toby's specialty. Look — there's old Mrs Stackett. Let's say hello.'

Our next-door neighbour, Mrs Stackett, saw us and waved excitedly.

'You know Ms Lefty, don't you, children? She's just telling me about her new hair-do. It's all the rage.'

Ms Penelope Lefty was from Community Welfare. She organised the Stacketts' Meals on Wheels and dropped in once a week to see how they were. Normally, Ms Lefty's hair was a crew cut dyed snow white. This time, though, she was growing little dreadlocks. They looked like the furballs Frankie's cat coughed up, stuck on her head.

'Very nice,' I said politely.

'It looks like the furballs Frankie's cat . . .' began Jasper.

I gave her a dig in the ribs to shut her up. Sometimes the truth wasn't necessary. Personally, I thought Ms Lefty looked like an armed robber minus the balaclava but I wasn't about to tell her that, either.

'And she's had her eyebrow pierced again, too,' said Mrs Stackett fondly. 'How many rings is that now, dear? Eight?'

'Nine, if you count the stud in my nose.' Ms Lefty smiled at us, her pierced bits winking in the sunlight.

I hoped for her sake that nobody went near her with a metal detector — it'd go off like a packet of crackers.

'I'm just making Mrs Stackett some sandwiches. Would you like to join us?'

'No, thanks. We're having lunch at Toby's,' said Jasper. 'Spag bol.'

Mrs Stackett chuckled. 'So that's what that

wonderful smell is. That boy is the best cook in Tumblegum Street. He beats me hands down!'

'Toby's cooking?' asked Ms Lefty.

'He always does,' Jasper boasted. 'He's a legend.'

Ms Lefty raised her eyebrow, the one with the two rings in it. 'How unusual. What does he cook?'

'Chicken satay, steak and salad, curried prawns . . .' I ticked the list off on my fingers. 'A different meal every night of the week and a roast on Sundays.'

'Every night of the week, you say?' Ms Lefty opened her folder and started writing in it.

'Without fail. I reckon they'd starve to death if he didn't!' said Jasper cheerfully. 'And so will we if we don't get going. Come on, Hugo.'

When I looked back over my shoulder, Ms Lefty had stopped writing. She was chewing her pen and staring thoughtfully at the Trotters' house.

Chapter Six

We were in a chat room on the Internet.

I looked nervously at Toby. This was like walking into a crowded room full of people talking over the top of each other. The only difference was, it was on the computer and people were talking to each other by writing messages.

Can you believe the guitar riffs on Mind Riot's latest album?

Totally awesome, aren't they?

You make me sad. Here in Germany is the album not yet out. My ears have not to its sound exploded.

> Well, what's wrong with your brain, Helmut
> Head? Get into the Net's CD megastore and
> download it . . . like now! Who needs a record
> store when you're on the Web?

I stared at the screen in wonder.

'This is what a chat room's all about,' Toby said.
'You can have real-time conversations with a whole
lot of people from all over the world.'

'They all seem to know each other,' I said. 'Do
you think they'd mind if I butted in to ask
questions about Mandy Miami?'

Toby shrugged. 'There's only one way to find out.'

Stalling for time, I re-read the sign at the top of
the screen.

> Welcome to the Rap Cafe. The ozone-friendly
> Internet chat zone for the exclusive use of
> Echo Records' customers, staff and stars. No
> spitting, no swearing and, please, keep your
> feet off the seats!

It was funny how it was called the Rap Cafe, as
though it was a real place where people sat around
drinking coffee and chatting. But it wasn't real, of
course. The Rap Cafe existed only in Cyberspace. It
was just a heap of people sitting at their computers
all over the world, talking to each other about a
common interest.

In this case the common interest was Echo Records.

'Well, I guess Papa Razzi knows what he's talking about.' I took a deep breath. What if nobody wanted to talk to me? 'Here goes.'

> SORRY TO INTERRUPT. DOES ANYONE HERE
> KNOW MANDY MIAMI?

There was a pause. I felt like I'd barged into a private conversation. Next thing I knew, people were yelling questions at me!

> Who wants to know?
>
> Who goes there? Sign thy name, oh nameless one.
>
> Is that the Shark again? If so, buzz off, bottom dweller!
>
> Stop shouting! Don't you know it's rude to write in capitals?

Toby read the replies over my shoulder.

'Oops, I forgot.' He tapped the keyboard. 'Only use small letters. If you write in capitals it means you're shouting. And you have to have a handle.'

I looked at him. 'A handle?'

'A nickname to sign your messages with.'

I thought back to my conversation with Papa Razzi.

> My name is Smart Alec· Sorry about the capitals, I just wanted to make sure you heard me. Who's the Shark?

My heart was pounding. I was in new territory here and I wasn't sure what to do next.

> The Shark is some aggro kid who was cruising here yesterday asking questions about Mandy.
>
> Too many questions.
>
> We didn't like the sound of him so we flamed him.

Flamed him? What were they talking about?

'They must have bombarded him with angry messages,' said Toby, reading my mind. 'That's what happens if you're rude on the Net.'

I shook my head. So many rules and I didn't know any of them. It wasn't just etiquette — it was Netiquette! And who was the Shark? Was there someone else on the same trail as us?

> Hey, Smart Alec!

This message sounded a little friendlier.

> Long time, no hear! You must be serious about this letter to Mandy, huh?

It was signed, Papa Razzi.

Papa Razzi! I felt a surge of relief. At least I knew one other person on-line. But before I could reply, the others jumped in.

> What letter?
>
> You know this geek, Papa? What's the story?

How do we know he's not the Shark?

The messages were flowing thick and fast. Papa Razzi jumped to my defense.

Relax, everyone, he's a friend of mine. A Mandy freak. From Australia. He's trying to get a message to her.

The others weren't impressed.

Join the queue, Smart Alec!

Someone else piped in:

Forget about Mandy, dude . . . Mind Riot's the way to go.

Ja!

I looked at Toby, bewildered. There were so many people in this conversation I couldn't hear myself think.

SHUT UP EVERYONE!

It was Papa Razzi again, shouting in capitals.

The Australian newbie has a genuine mission to deliver Mandy a letter. Can anyone help?

Now that Papa Razzi had stuck up for me, the others seemed to back off.

The only one who can help is the Joker,

suggested someone.

Yeah. The Joker knows Mandy personally.

> He's a friend of hers. That's what he reckons.

> Nah! I bet he works for Echo Records. That's why he knows so much. And why else would he spend so much time in the chat room?

The Rap Cafe was abuzz. I read the messages eagerly. A clue! Someone called the Joker had contact with Mandy — or so he said. After all, he was called the Joker. Still, it was worth a try.

> Sorry to interrupt again. It's Smart Alec here. Can anyone tell me how to contact the Joker?

Silence. Nobody answered. Even Papa Razzi was lost for words. Maybe they still didn't trust me. Or maybe nobody knew. It seemed like the Net had taken me through a twisting, turning maze of pathways — only to throw me up against a dead end.

Suddenly, someone spoke.

> Ah, so nice to see someone with manners among this quarrelsome rabble! Name your mission and your purpose, dear boy. And don't forget to include a joke for my collection.

It was the Joker. He'd been listening the whole time.

The minutes ticked by. Toby checked his watch.

'Thirty-five minutes. If the Joker was able to get the letter to Mandy, surely we would have heard by now.'

While we waited, I tried hard to get a picture of the

Joker in my mind. He sounded older than the others in the Rap Cafe and more formal. For some reason, the image of an old English gentleman with a bowler hat and a walking stick, sipping a cup of tea, jumped into my mind.

I stared at the computer screen glumly. Somewhere on the other side of the world, that old English gentleman had my precious letter to Mandy. Everyone else in the chat room had lost interest. They'd moved on to other singers, other questions.

The Joker hadn't spoken now for more than half an hour, ever since I'd E-mailed the letter to him. Maybe he hated my joke. For the fifteenth time, I went over it in my head. *What goes pedal, pedal, crash! A dork on a bicycle.* All right, so it wasn't very funny. But it was the best I could do under pressure.

Toby nudged me. 'Hey! He's back.'

I sat up, rubbing my eyes. These late nights were killing me.

> Bravo, Smart Alec! For once, a joke I haven't heard before! I assure you I laughed until I wept. I took the liberty of placing it in my Cyber-gallery of Jests, Gags and Ribticklers, accessed by hundreds of intrepid Web travellers each day.

Phew! What a good thing I hadn't used my other joke, about the chicken crossing the road. He'd probably heard it already.

I quickly replied.

> I'm honoured. But what about the letter?

> Yeah! What about the letter, Jokey-baby!

That was Papa Razzi, butting back into the conversation. He didn't miss a trick. He was even more of a stickybeak than Jasper and that was really saying something.

> Ah yes, the letter.

The Joker paused.

> I have passed the letter on to my good friend Mandy Miami. At least, I have left it in her mailbox, where I presume she will read it at her leisure. Possibly when she returns from her Australian tour.

After her tour — but that was too late! Toby and I looked at each other, horrified.

> My humble thanks . . . but this is urgent, Joker. I need to contact Mandy straightaway,

I wrote frantically.

> I know, dear fellow. I couldn't help but read some of your letter as I mailed it on. You and your friends *are* in a spot of bother, aren't you?

I answered:

> It's a total nightmare. I'm trying as hard as I can to find Mandy but I just keep running into dead

ends. If only I could speak to her . . . or, at least, find out when she's arriving in Australia.

The Rap Cafe was silent. I realised that everyone else had stopped talking and was listening to my conversation with the Joker.

I know the information you seek. But sadly, my friend, it is confidential. A good friendship cannot be betrayed on the whim of a stranger — no matter how honourable that stranger is.

I wrote back:

Just a clue. Nothing more — just a clue about where I can find Mandy when she gets to Australia.

There was a long pause. It was like everyone in the Rap Cafe was holding their breath.

A clue? Well, a clue is another matter,

wrote the Joker eventually.

The thing is, dear boy, do you have another joke to trade for it?

I thought quickly.

Sure. We have a teacher at school called Mrs McSmell. It takes a lot to upset her. The other day, a 747 jet crashed into our classroom and she said, 'Who threw that?'

Toby snorted with laughter. 'Good one, Hugo!'

But I wasn't listening. My eyes were glued to the computer screen.

> Capital! A quick laugh at short notice. For that, you earn the first half of the clue. Are you ready?

Ready? I was turning purple with impatience. Finally, the Joker wrote:

> *A bird that can't fly/comes down from the sky/ on a baker's dozen day/when the moon is away.*

A bird that can't fly? I looked at Toby — but he was busy writing it down on a piece of paper.

> It doesn't make sense,

I wrote back. Poetry's never been my best subject.

> You'd better give me the second half.

The Joker replied:

> Not so fast, old fruit.

I got the impression he was enjoying this.

> If you concentrate, you'll see it makes perfect sense. But I'm quite happy to divulge the second half — for a price. You know the rules.

'I haven't got another joke,' I told Toby desperately. 'I can't think.'

Toby patted my shoulder. 'Relax.' He reached in front of me and tapped out something on the keyboard.

What do you call an Australian animal that gets squashed by a truck? A duck-billed splattypus!

I could almost hear the Joker chortling.

Excellent, young friend! I like the Australian flavour! So dinkum, as you say. Very well, here is the second part of your clue:

'The path from A to B / is sometimes via C and D / and when you don't know where to turn / remember, it's the early bird that catches the worm!

I groaned. That didn't explain anything. In fact, it just made it more confusing.

Toby finished writing. He read what he'd copied down and shook his head. 'Makes no sense to me. But let's sleep on it. We'll call a meeting in the morning and try to work it out.'

My heart sank. How could you work out something that didn't make sense? What on earth was a baker's dozen day? What sort of a bird didn't fly? And what did the letters A, B, C and D have to do with Mandy Miami?

I made my way home in the dark with the words of the puzzle buzzing through my brain.

And as I fell into a troubled sleep, I thought I heard the Joker laughing at me.

Chapter Seven

'I reckon he's just a crazy old coot who's pulling your leg.' Jasper barged through the door of the Cave and flopped into one of the couches, scowling.

Toby and I didn't answer. We'd been poring over the Joker's puzzle all morning and, although neither of us wanted to admit it, we'd started to reach the same conclusion ourselves.

'It may as well be in French,' Toby sighed. 'We'd have just as much chance of understanding it.'

'Or Ancient Greek,' I added sadly.

'Or Swahili,' suggested Jasper, trying to make me laugh. It didn't work. My brain was starting to ache and, as I stared at the computer, a wave of anger swept over me. How dare the Joker play such a mean trick on us!

'It's not fair!' I yelled.

Toby and Jasper jumped. I picked up a cushion and flung it at Myron as hard as I could, imagining that I was throwing it at an old English gentleman with a bowler hat and a walking stick.

'Hey! Take it easy!' Toby grabbed my arm as I went to pick up another cushion.

'Jasper's right, he's just playing with us,' I said angrily. 'All that stuff about birds and worms and the moon . . . there's no connection at all between any of it!' I slumped into a chair, defeated.

Toby looked at me thoughtfully. 'You know, you're absolutely right,' he said slowly. 'There's no connection at all . . . Hugo, I think you've just made a breakthrough.'

I looked at him grumpily. The only thing I felt like breaking was the Joker's head.

'Don't you see, that's the mistake we've been making!' said Toby excitedly. 'Trying to make sense of the puzzle as one complete thing. In fact, it's probably a whole lot of little clues strung together to look like a poem!'

He jumped up and grabbed the piece of paper with the Joker's puzzle on it. 'Let's give it one more go.'

'A bird that can't fly,
Comes down from the sky,
On a baker's dozen day,
When the moon is away,
The path from A to B,
Is sometimes better via C and D,
And when you don't know where to turn,
Remember, it's the early bird that catches the worm!'

'It sounds the same to me,' I shrugged. 'Gibberish. A load of rot. Gobbledygook.'

Toby was pacing the floor, muttering under his breath.

'Line by line,' I heard him say. 'We have to dissect it, line by line.'

'Dissect it?' Now *that* I understood. 'You mean like that frog in science class?'

'Exactly!' Toby stopped pacing. 'Let's figure out what the first little bit means . . . forget about the rest, we'll do that later.'

'A bird that can't fly,' mused Jasper. 'It still doesn't make sense, Toby. There's no such thing as a bird that can't fly. That's what birds *do*, for heaven's sake.'

Something was nagging in the back of my mind. Something about a flightless bird . . . a big flightless bird.

'A dodo?' I asked tentatively. 'Is there such a thing as a dodo?'

'There's one sitting in your chair. Oh, it's you.'
Jasper fell about laughing at her own joke.

'Actually, you're right, Hugo,' said Toby, ignoring her. 'Hundreds of years ago, there was a bird called a dodo that couldn't fly. But it's extinct. It died out years ago.'

So the dodo was extinct — but at least we'd proved one thing. The Joker's puzzle wasn't complete nonsense.

'Hey, how about an ostrich?' Jasper stopped laughing and sat up on the couch. 'Is an ostrich a bird?'

'Sure is,' said Toby jubilantly, writing it down. 'It's a bird that *doesn't fly*. Now we're on the right track!'

The thought I'd been waiting for suddenly hit me. 'An emu!' We'd learned about emus at school and I remembered seeing one at the wildlife sanctuary. It had a long neck, haughty eyes and big sharp claws. 'Emus don't fly!'

Toby's eyes were shining. He wrote it down. 'See! I told you we'd crack this code!'

'It still doesn't mean anything — yet,' I reminded him. 'Don't forget the next bit. *A bird that can't fly comes down from the sky*. If it can't fly, what's it doing up in the sky? It couldn't get there on its own.'

'Unless it was in an aeroplane,' joked Jasper. 'Emu up in first class.'

I started to laugh, then I stopped. A bird and an aeroplane . . . I looked at Toby and I could see he was thinking the same thing.

'EMU AIRLINES!' we both shouted.

Before I knew it, the three of us had jumped up and were dancing around the room with excitement.

'Mandy Miami's arriving on Emu Airlines!' I said. 'That's the only thing it could possibly mean. The Joker wasn't playing a trick on us!'

Toby stopped, puffing.

'Don't get too excited — we've still got the rest of the puzzle to work out. We don't know what day she's arriving, for example.'

'Yes, we do,' said Jasper. 'We know the exact day.'

Toby and I looked at her, mystified.

She snatched the poem from Toby and pointed at the next line. 'A . . . baker's . . . dozen . . . day!'

'But what on earth is that?' asked Toby. 'I've got no idea what a baker's dozen is.'

Jasper grabbed our hands and pulled us towards the door. 'Let's go and ask Great-aunt Miranda. She's as old as the hills. I bet she knows. Come on!'

I felt like I was caught up in a whirlwind. We ran all the way to Great-aunt Miranda's and flew in the door just as she was taking out a steaming batch of fresh scones from the oven.

'My, my, what a lovely surprise,' she clucked. 'Just in time for afternoon tea . . .'

'Great-aunt Miranda, what's a baker's dozen?' demanded Jasper, interrupting her.

'Well . . . heavens . . . A baker's dozen is when the baker pops an extra cake or bun into the bag when you order a dozen,' replied Great-aunt Miranda, looking a little flustered. 'It's been such a long time since I . . .'

'So you get thirteen instead of twelve?' Toby asked urgently.

'Well, yes, dear — as long as you can find a baker these days who . . .'

'A baker's dozen is thirteen, Hugo,' Toby said to me. 'Write that down. What's the date today?'

'The twelfth of January. Why?' I asked.

Great-aunt Miranda looked totally confused. 'Children, children . . . what's this all about?'

'We've got no time to lose,' ordered Toby. 'Let's get out of here.'

'But . . . but . . . you've only just . . . Oh, my hat and feathers!'

'Thanks, Great-aunt Miranda,' said Jasper, planting a big kiss on her cheek as she flew out the door.

'Thanks, Great-aunt Miranda,' I said, giving her a big bear hug that nearly knocked her over.

'Yes ... er ... thanks, Great-aunt Miranda,' said Toby, grabbing her hand and shaking it very formally.

I tapped him on the shoulder as we jogged back to the Cave. 'Hey. She's not your great-aunt.'

Toby grinned. '*I* know that and *you* know that. But in all the rush, I don't think Great-aunt Miranda would have noticed!'

After that, the rest of the puzzle almost fell into place by itself. When we checked the calender for the phases of the moon, January thirteenth was marked with a black circle.

'The new moon,' nodded Toby. 'Just as I suspected. The one day of the month where you can't see the moon.'

A baker's dozen day when the moon is away ...

'Where does the moon go, just out of interest?' I asked.

'Nowhere. It's still there. We just can't see it because the sun's light isn't reflecting off it. It's the one time of the month that the Earth gets in the way.'

Now that the puzzle was starting to make sense, I was feeling a lot friendlier towards the Joker. Still, he hadn't given us much time. If his information was correct, Mandy was arriving on Emu Airlines on January thirteenth. That was the next day!

I got onto the Internet and accessed the Emu Airlines home page. I had a hunch that at least one of the other clues would help us find out the exact flight Mandy would be on. We needed to know the flight timetables.

'There's something that's bothering me.' I clicked into the JAN 13 flight schedule. 'How does the Joker know so much about Mandy?'

Toby shrugged. 'Like they said in the Rap Cafe, he probably works for Echo Records. You know what computer geeks are like . . . they get into everything. He probably browses through all their internal memos and private mailboxes on his lunch break.'

That made sense. The Joker claimed he was a friend of Mandy's — but like Toby said, he was more likely some small-time hacker. People like the Joker got a kick out of digging up secret information. Passing it on to other people was their way of getting recognition for their skills.

'I've got it!' I beckoned Toby over.

Jasper had already gone — now that we'd cracked the Joker's code, Jasper had her own story to work on. She was on her way to the Municipal Library to check the electoral rolls for Lindsay Bishop. That was a tip we'd picked up from Toby's dad. As soon as you turn eighteen, he said, your name and address goes on a big rollbook. Then, at election time, the government could make sure you'd voted. But it was also a good way for reporters and private detectives to find people. If only it was that easy to find Mandy Miami!

'Look.' I pointed at the long list of flights that Emu Airlines had coming in from all over the world. 'There's only one direct flight from Los Angeles to Sydney. It arrives at ten o'clock in the morning. That has to be the one Mandy's on.'

'Easy!' crowed Toby. Then his face fell. 'Almost too easy. Every reporter in Australia will be trying to work out which flight she's on. Why would she be so obvious?'

Hmmm . . . Toby had a good point. On the other hand, unless Mandy hopped on a magic carpet, she didn't have too many choices.

'She's a busy person,' I shrugged. 'She's got to get from A to B as quickly as possible, I guess she . . .'

I stopped dead in my tracks.

'*The path from A to B is sometimes better via C and D*,' recited Toby slowly. 'Hugo, you're a genius. Check if there are any flights that aren't direct.'

There were two. Both went from Los Angeles to Hawaii to New Zealand and then to Sydney.

'When Dad went to America to report on the Olympics, he made sure he got a direct flight,' Toby said. 'These other ones take forever. That's why people don't like them.'

If that was the case, who would ever suspect that a famous pop star would catch one? It was a perfect cover!

'One arrives at eight o'clock in the morning — the other one comes in at ten o'clock at night,' I told Toby, checking the schedule. 'I wonder which one it is? I can't spend the whole day and night at the airport — I'd never get away with it!'

Toby didn't even bother answering. He just picked up the piece of paper with the Joker's poem on it and pointed to the last two lines.

Of course. I'd be setting my alarm for very, very early the next morning. Like the Joker said, it's the early bird that catches the worm.

'Mandy Miami's arriving on Emu Airlines Flight 123, tomorrow morning at eight o'clock!'

It was definitely Frankie's voice but so muffled I could hardly hear her. It sounded like she was calling from the bottom of a mine shaft in the middle of a cyclone.

'I rang as soon as Howard told me. His mum's letting him take her limousine and chauffeur. They're going to pick me up at seven on the way to the airport.'

'What!' I was flabbergasted. How on earth had Howard found out? After all the trouble that Jasper, Toby and I had gone to working out the Joker's clues, it didn't seem fair.

'Howard's got contacts.' Frankie's voice was thin and faint, barely audible above the static and wailing noises on the phone line. 'I think he might have bribed somebody to tell him. He's absolutely sure the information is right.'

'Where are you?' I asked.

'In the linen cupboard,' came the muted reply. 'I'm on the portable phone. I don't want anyone to hear me talking to you. If Howard finds out I'm still working for *Street Wise* . . .' Her voice trailed off.

Frustrated, I wished Frankie was over at my place so we could talk properly. But ever since she'd taken the job with Howard, she'd had to keep right away from us so he didn't suspect anything.

'I'll see you at the airport tomorrow,' I heard Frankie say from the bottom of the coal mine. 'Eight o'clock. Flight 123. Don't be late!'

I hung up and went to get the bus timetable. Frankie and Howard might be going to the airport in style — but for this chief reporter, it was going to be good old public transport.

As I walked past Jasper's room, I heard the computer give a double beep. Incoming mail.

I clicked on the flashing mailbox, expecting a message from Toby. But it wasn't. In fact, there was no way of telling who it was from. It was an anonymous E-mail, sent through a central Internet address so there was no way of tracing the sender.

The message was just one line.

Watch out for red herrings.

Chapter Eight

I set the alarm and slipped quietly out of the house at 6.30 am the next morning, leaving my bedroom door shut so Mum and Dad would think I was still asleep. I knew I could trust Jasper to come up with an alibi for me if she had to. 'Working on the newspaper' was a good one — they would automatically assume I was in the Cave with Toby, who was busy laying out the newspaper and putting headlines on the stories we'd already done. And if that failed — well, it didn't really matter because by then, I'd be interviewing Mandy Miami for my world exclusive story!

BARP-BARP! BARP-BARP!

I nearly jumped out of my skin as a giant black limousine skidded to a halt next to me, its horn blasting. Howard Fitzherbert wound down the window, smirking.

'Sorry, we don't pick up hitch-hikers! Drive on, Allenby! Ha, ha, ha!'

His mocking laughter floated back to me as the limo roared off, blowing a cloud of dust in my face. Coughing and spluttering, I made my way to the bus stop.

As the old bus jolted and clattered its way into the city, my mind was buzzing. How did Howard find out Mandy Miami's flight? Was it a tip-off from one of his family's well-connected friends, as Frankie said? Or had he somehow stolen the information from us? And who was the anonymous person who had sent me the message? *Watch out for red herrings.* A red herring was a false clue . . . something to trick you or distract you from the real thing. Why would someone send me a message like that?

About five kilometres down the road, I was pleased to see the big black limousine pulled over with its bonnet up. Mrs Allenby, the chauffeur, was leaning against the car fanning her face with her cap. Howard was yelling into his mobile phone and Frankie was sitting by the side of the road fiddling with her cameras. Well, that was something,

I thought as the bus chugged past. Maybe Howard wouldn't get there first after all!

I'd never been to the airport before. When the bus pulled up outside I nearly fell off my seat with shock. So many people! There were millions of them, rushing in and out of the doors, lugging suitcases and looking at their watches. Hundreds of travellers squashed onto the escalator going up, and hundreds more squashed onto the other escalator going down. Big bunches of people clustered around a conveyor belt with suitcases on it. They were pushing and shoving each other to get to their bags.

'National Airlines Flight 679 departing now from Gate 7,' boomed a voice over a loudspeaker. 'Flying Kangaroo Flight 222 arriving now at Gate 23 . . .'

I stood there with my mouth open taking it all in. It was like the Easter Show without the rides and the animal smells. How on earth was I going to find Mandy Miami in the middle of all this?

'Catching flies, are you son?' I jumped out of the way. It was a porter wheeling a trolley piled sky-high with bags and suitcases. He grinned at me. 'Not lost are you?'

I thought quickly. 'No, I'm meeting a friend. She's on Emu Airlines Flight 123. Can you tell me where to go?'

The porter kept walking but he jerked his head in the direction of a big television screen with writing on it. 'See that? It's got all the arrivals and departures on it. Tells you what gate to go to. Then just follow the signs.'

I thanked him and checked the board. Emu Airlines Flight 123 from Los Angeles via Hawaii and Auckland was arriving at Gate 27 at 8.05 am. I checked my watch — 7.55 am. The plane was running five minutes late. That should give me plenty of time to find Gate 27. I squeezed onto the escalator and rode to the top wedged between a big woman in a floral dress and an old man with hair sprouting from his ears and his nostrils. Luckily it was a short trip.

At the top of the escalator I tried to fight my way out of the crowd but it was impossible, so I gave up. Everyone else seemed to know where they were going better than I did, anyway. All of a sudden I felt the ground moving beneath my feet. I looked down. Yikes! I was gliding along on what looked like a flat escalator.

'These people-movers are a great idea, Marge,' I heard the old man with whiskery ears say.

'Lordy, lordy, it's nice to rest my feet,' the big woman in the flowery dress replied. 'You hang onto the railing tight now, Pop, and don't move!'

A people-mover — cool! This was even better than the Easter Show. I was starting to enjoy myself.

Once I got used to the strange sensation of gliding along without walking, I let go of the rail and started experimenting. Taking steps while the ground was moving beneath me was like walking on air. Every step I took I moved forward two metres! It was like being Superman. Or if I slowed down, like being an astronaut. For a while I pretended I was walking on the moon. Then I sped up.

'Hugo Lilley in lane five, representing Australia,' I muttered under my breath, starting to jog. 'Yes, folks, it's no wonder this boy has reached the Olympics at such a young age . . . he makes it all look so easy!'

'Watch it, sonny!' barked a woman with bright yellow hair. 'You'll knock the cameras.'

Cameras? That snapped me out of it. I took another look at the woman. It was Marilyn Miller, the glamorous TV reporter from Channel Five in Blue Rock. She was standing next to a man with a video camera on his shoulder and another man loaded up with floodlights and other equipment. What were they doing here?

I dropped out of the Olympic race and stood quietly in front of the TV crew. The gold medal could wait.

'Are you sure we need to get here so early, Marilyn?' asked one of the men. 'Her plane doesn't arrive for another two hours.'

'Are you crazy?' screeched Marilyn. 'Every reporter in Australia will be here soon. I want you to set up the cameras right at the front before everyone else gets here. I want the best spot . . . OR ELSE!'

I turned my head casually towards them and saw the cameraman roll his eyes at the assistant. Marilyn was busy putting powder all over her face.

'If I can get an interview with Mandy Miami, the big networks will be fighting to give me a job,' Marilyn said, pouting at herself in the compact mirror. '*Adios*, Blue Rock! Come on, boys . . . here's Gate 24.'

So they were trying to find Mandy Miami too! I watched as the crew stepped off the people-mover and headed towards Gate 24. It looked like there were already some other reporters there as well. I stayed where I was and watched them fade into the distance. Marilyn and the other reporters didn't know it, but they were at the wrong gate. Just as we'd suspected, they all thought that Mandy would arrive on a direct flight. Thank goodness for the Joker!

A large crowd of people were already waiting at Gate 27 by the time I got there. None of them looked like reporters or fans. Good. With any luck I'd have this story all to myself.

Suddenly a familiar voice broke into my thoughts.

'Greetings, maggot brain.'

I turned around. It was Howard. Frankie was behind him, putting a film into her camera. Without looking at me, she gave me our secret sign — a thumbs up. I noticed she'd drawn a smiley on her thumb with black ink.

'Nice to see you again, Howard,' I replied coldly, 'NOT!'

Frankie snapped the camera closed and joined us. 'The car broke down,' she said. 'Howard had to call the mechanic to put a new fan belt in it.'

Howard turned on her. 'I told you not to talk to him! You work for me now,' he said angrily.

Frankie shrugged and walked away. When Howard turned his back she went cross-eyed and stuck her tongue out at him. I had to pinch myself so I didn't laugh.

'Well, it looks like we're both here for the same reason,' I said.

'With one difference.' Howard smirked. 'I'm going to get the interview with Mandy Miami. You're not.'

A hot wave of anger swept through me but I clenched my fists and stayed calm. That rat Howard wasn't going to get the better of me! Besides, there was something I wanted to know.

'How did you find out she was arriving on this flight?'

Howard laughed nastily. 'Maybe I got Frankie to steal the information from you.'

I shook my head. 'Frankie's not like that. Although I wouldn't put it past *you*.' I baited the line and threw it out. 'You're not smart enough to find out yourself.'

'Is that right?' replied Howard furiously, taking the bait. 'Well, as a matter of fact, I'm a lot smarter than you are! I got the Joker's clues without even asking for them, so there!'

I looked at him sceptically. We'd had to work hard for those clues. How could Howard get hold of them without asking?

'It's the Internet, dummy!' Howard laughed scornfully seeing my look. 'Or should I call you Smart Alec?'

A horrible suspicion was starting to dawn on me.

'Anyone can listen in to those chat rooms,' continued Howard. 'I just had to wait for you to come along and do all the work for me.'

Of course! I thumped my forehead.

'You're out of your depth on the Internet, Hugo,' said Howard in a sinister voice. 'And you know what they say about deep water ... watch out for shark attacks.'

Shark attacks! All of a sudden it made sense. Howard was the Shark! He'd been lying in wait, knowing we'd eventually find our way to the chat room ...

I didn't have a chance to think about it anymore. The doors of the arrival lounge swung open and people started pouring out. And right at the front was a girl who looked exactly like a pop star.

She was small and slim, and dressed completely in red — a tight red top that didn't cover her belly-button and tight red pants. Just like Mandy, she had long, brown hair all the way down her back. I couldn't see her face, because she was wearing big black sunglasses and a red hat — but it had to be Mandy. What were the chances of having two pop stars on the same flight?

'That's her!' yelled Howard. 'Come on, Frankie!'

The girl in red looked startled as Howard charged towards her, pushing people aside.

'Out of my way!' bellowed Howard, knocking over a baby that was standing there sucking its thumb. The baby sat down hard on its bottom and started screaming.

'Hey, you!' The baby's father shook his fist at Howard. 'What's all this commotion?'

The girl's expression changed from surprise to alarm. She watched as Howard sprinted towards her with Frankie hot on his heels. She saw the camera. And then, she started to run.

'After her!' Howard ordered. He grabbed Frankie by the jumper and the two of them took off in hot pursuit.

'Hurry up, Hugo!' whispered Frankie as she rushed past. 'This is your big chance.'

'Quick! She's ducking out a side entrance!' Howard was on his mobile phone, frantically dialling. 'Allenby! Take the limousine round the back of the airport and block off all the exits. Get some cab drivers to help you — pay them whatever they want. Don't let her get away!'

As I watched the girl in red struggling to open an emergency exit door, I heard what sounded like a herd of buffaloes thundering down the corridor. It was the pack of reporters from Gate 24. They must have heard the ruckus and twigged that something was up.

'It's Mandy Miami!' one of them shouted as they stormed past in a tangle of electrical cords and microphones. 'She's tricked us again!'

For some reason I couldn't move. It was like my feet were stuck to the ground with superglue. I just stood there like a lump of wood, hanging onto my notebook and pen, and watching as Howard, Frankie and the rampaging horde of reporters streamed through the door after Mandy.

'Well, aren't you going to join them?' I turned around. It was the last of the passengers to come through the door — a little old lady. Her eyes twinkled at me. 'You're a reporter too, aren't you? I can tell by the notebook.'

'I thought I was.' I stared sadly at the closed door. Somewhere out there, somebody — probably Howard — was getting my exclusive interview with Mandy Miami. 'But I mustn't be a very good one. I don't want to chase somebody like that. It's horrible. I want someone to talk to me because they want to.'

The old lady chuckled. 'Sounds to me like that's the way to get the best interviews.'

I watched glumly as she walked jauntily onto the people-mover, swinging her tartan bag. Maybe she was right. But that didn't help me now.

Then I took another look. There was something about the old lady that wasn't quite right. It wasn't the grey hair or the glasses . . . it was something else. It wasn't until she was a long way away that it finally clicked.

It was the way she was walking.

It wasn't the way an old person walked, slowly and carefully so they wouldn't fall over, especially on a people-mover. I remembered the old man with hair growing out of his ears. 'Hang on tight, Pop and don't move,' his daughter had said. This old lady was sauntering along without even holding on.

'That's not an old lady,' I said to myself. 'That's somebody a lot younger disguised as an old lady.'

The anonymous E-mail message suddenly popped into my head.

Watch out for red herrings.

Red herrings . . . red . . . the girl who looked like a pop star had been dressed in red.

I strained my eyes and caught a final glimpse of the old lady gliding off into the distance.

'Excuse me . . . wait! Please wait!'

I jumped onto the people-mover and started running.

Chapter Nine

'I missed her.' I threw myself onto Jasper's bed and groaned. 'I can't believe I was *this close* . . .' I held up my thumb and forefinger a whisker apart, '. . . and she disappeared.'

'Join the club. I feel like a failure too.' Jasper sat cross-legged on the floor looking miserable. 'No Lindsay Bishop on the electoral rolls and none in the phone book either. I must have rung twenty L. Bishops. Plenty of Lindas and Larrys, but no Lindsays.'

I heard the trellis bumping against the outside wall, then Frankie's face appeared above the window sill.

'Oh, good, I hoped you'd be home.'

She clambered through the open window.

'What's wrong? You both look terrible.'

'I can't find the new teacher,' said Jasper mournfully. 'That means no story — and no girlfriend for Toby's dad!'

'And I can't find Mandy Miami,' I added.

Frankie listened sympathetically. 'Well, look on the bright side. Howard didn't find Mandy either. That girl turned out to be a decoy. When she took off the hat and sunglasses, she didn't look anything like Mandy Miami. Howard was furious.'

So my hunch had been right. But what was Frankie doing here? 'Aren't you worried Howard might see you?' I asked.

Frankie shook her head. 'It doesn't matter anymore. I quit.'

Jasper perked up a little. 'You *quit*? Well, come on . . . tell us the gory details!'

'There's not a lot to tell. I thought it was awful the way Howard chased that girl down. She must have felt like a trapped animal. That's not how I want to get my photographs. So I quit.' She grinned at us. 'Of course, I waited until we got back to Blue Rock. I didn't want to walk home from the airport.'

Good old Frankie! It was great to have her back. But it still didn't solve our problem — we had a newspaper to put out and no front page story.

Jasper jumped up. 'Come on. Let's go to the Cave

and tell Toby. He's the editor. The sooner we tell him, the sooner he can come up with a solution.'

I followed with a heavy heart. Somehow, I knew Toby wasn't going to be too happy with the news.

But Toby wasn't there. The Cave was empty.

'That's funny,' I said. 'This close to deadline Toby usually sleeps and eats here.'

I rifled through the papers on the desk. They were the proofs — the practice runs — of our regular features like Dr Death and the social pages. There was a half-written headline on the computer screen: 'Last Days of Freedom, It's Back to Sch ...' Toby had obviously dropped everything in a hurry. What could be so important that he wouldn't even finish the word he was typing?

'Let's try the house.' Jasper sounded puzzled too.

We heard the raised voices even before we reached the back door. There were people inside, shouting at each other.

'. . . can't you just leave us alone . . . we're perfectly happy,' I heard Mr Trotter say.

Then a woman's voice, not as loud, but very firm. '. . . only doing my job . . . regulations . . .'

I cupped my hands around my eyes and peered through the screen door. 'It's Ms Lefty!' I whispered. 'She's arguing with Mr Trotter. Toby's in there too.'

Jasper pushed me out of the way. 'Here. Let me see.'

Frankie squirmed in under Jasper's arm. 'Yeah. Shove over.'

We were so busy trying to stickybeak we didn't notice the door wasn't shut properly. Somebody leaned too hard on it, the door opened suddenly, and the next thing I knew the three of us had fallen forward and landed in a big tangled heap on the Trotter's kitchen floor!

Well, that certainly stopped the argument in its tracks.

'Good heavens, it's the press gallery!' Mr Trotter laughed weakly and patted his forehead with a big red hanky. He looked almost relieved to see us. 'Ms Lefty and I were just having a . . . little talk.'

Toby looked pale and anxious. He shot me a worried look and gave the 'thumbs down' signal. Something bad was going on.

Ms Lefty smiled at us but when she turned back to Mr Trotter her face was stern again.

'Mr Trotter, we have to sort this out. I have a report — confirmed by a number of people — that your eleven-year-old son is the primary caregiver in this household.'

'The primary school caretaker?' Jasper butted in. 'No, he's not. That's old Mr Fish. He's been there for years and —'

'Quiet, please,' said Ms Lefty. 'Mr Trotter, this is not acceptable. A child that is forced to cook and do the grocery shopping is not receiving proper parenting.' She paused, then added gently, 'We may have to consider fostering Toby to a family that has more time to look after him.'

'Foster him out? To another family?' Mr Trotter's face turned white. He looked like he was about to faint. 'But *I'm* his family. This is his home . . .'

'I'm not forced to cook and shop, Ms Lefty,' Toby burst out. 'I like to do it. It's me and Dad, pitching in together.'

Ms Lefty shook her head. 'I've also heard he works late at night putting out a newspaper. This is no life for a child, Mr Trotter. You must see that.'

I couldn't keep quiet any longer. Neither could Jasper.

'But Ms Lefty, it's our newspaper too!'

'It's not just work, it's fun!'

Ms Lefty fidgeted with one of her eyebrow rings. 'Well, he still shouldn't be looking after his father. It's supposed to be the other way around.' But she didn't sound as certain.

Mr Trotter's long lanky frame suddenly crumpled. He sat down at the kitchen table and put his head in his hands. Toby went over and patted him on the back. He looked at Ms Lefty defiantly.

'I know I do a lot of the cooking, Ms Lefty. But that's only because I want to be as good as my dad. He taught me everything I know.' He turned to Jasper and Frankie and me. 'Isn't that right?'

I looked sideways at Jasper. We both knew Mr Trotter couldn't make a piece of toast without burning it. The last time he tried he almost set the house on fire.

'Absolutely,' lied Jasper cheerfully. 'Mr Trotter is a brilliant cook.' She kicked me. 'Isn't he, Hugo?'

'Er . . . yes,' I stammered. 'Good enough to work in a restaurant.' I had a sudden burst of inspiration. 'In fact, he *did* work in a restaurant.'

'He was a famous chef before he was a reporter,' added Frankie eagerly. 'My dad took photographs of him for a magazine. He won heaps of awards.'

Mr Trotter stared at us as if we'd gone mad. But luckily, he kept his mouth shut.

Ms Lefty looked perplexed — and rather impressed. 'Is this true?' she asked Mr Trotter.

Mr Trotter opened his mouth to speak, but Toby butted in before he could say anything.

'Of course it's true, Ms Lefty,' he said. 'And what's more, we'll prove it to you.'

Ms Lefty raised a pierced eyebrow. 'Prove it?'

Mr Trotter mopped his brow with the red hanky again. 'How?' he asked faintly.

Toby turned to Ms Lefty and bowed politely. 'Please honour us with your company tomorrow night. Dinner will be served at seven-thirty.'

Ms Lefty frowned. 'This is most irregular . . . and how do I know . . .'

Toby interrupted. 'You are welcome to arrive earlier, of course.' He glanced at his father. 'To watch the master chef at work.'

'Great,' I grumbled as I typed my password into Myron. 'Just when I need Toby's help, he has to give his father a crash course in gourmet cooking.'

'Well, it's better than letting Ms Lefty take him away to a foster home,' Frankie pointed out.

Jasper flicked her plaits and sat down beside me. 'Anyway, I'll help you. Now that my story's fallen through, I've got nothing better to do.'

'Gee, thanks a million,' I said sarcastically. Jasper's idea of 'helping' usually meant 'completely taking over'.

'Now, I think the first thing you should do is contact the Joker.' She prodded me. 'Come on. What are you waiting for?'

I sighed. There didn't seem to be much point. The Joker had already given us some good clues and we'd wasted them. Correction — *I'd* wasted them. Mandy Miami had been right under my nose and I hadn't even realised it. He'd probably be angry with me. Or worse, he'd think I was stupid.

'Stop feeling sorry for yourself,' ordered Jasper. 'The Joker's the only one who might know where Mandy is now that she's in Australia. What have you got to lose?'

Maybe she was right. Glumly, I accessed the Rap Cafe. Personally, I'd be surprised if anyone was there at this hour — except for another Australian. Over in America or England, it was probably the middle of the night.

To my surprise, the Joker was on-line. Strange . . . it was almost as though he'd been waiting for us.

> Greetings young friend! How nice to speak to you again. Had a little bad luck at the airport, I hear?

I started to reply, then a thought struck me. What if the Shark was listening in again? We weren't the only ones still looking for Mandy Miami.

Frankie read my mind. 'I'll go and distract Howard,' she said, slipping out the door. 'Don't worry, I'll keep him occupied. Just give me five minutes.'

I strung out my story about the airport until I thought the coast was clear. Then I got to the point.

> We've got a problem,

I told the Joker.

The boy who is trying to run us out of business is the Shark. He wants to find Mandy as well and he was listening in to our last conversation. We need more clues to find Mandy and we need them now because we know he's not on-line.

I re-read the message. It sounded almost rude. But we were racing against time. I had no idea how long Frankie could keep Howard away from his computer. If he suspected anything was up . . .

So you're asking me to tell you where Mandy is hiding?

The Joker's message was as blunt as mine.

We've got nowhere else to turn.

I didn't want to beg, but I was getting close.

My dear boy, that sort of information is top secret. You're asking for a miracle.

I know.

The Joker sounded like he was getting annoyed.

Well, this is a chat room, not a miracle motel. Maybe you should try there.

I gave it one last try.

Just one more clue? Anything. Make it as hard as you want.

There was a long silence. Finally, the Joker answered.

> You already have the answer. Everything you
> need to know is on the Internet. That is all I
> have to say. Good luck.

I groaned and thumped Myron. The Joker wasn't making any sense at all. If I already knew the answer, I wouldn't be sitting here tearing my hair out.

'Think.' Jasper closed her eyes and pressed her forefingers to her temples. 'He says everything you need to know is on the Internet. Is there anything you've found out about Mandy Miami on the Web? Something you've forgotten?'

I racked my brains. It seemed like years since I had crept out of bed in the dead of night to start my search on the Internet.

'There's not a lot of information about Mandy anywhere,' I said helplessly. 'Including the Web. She's only ever done one interview and that was years ago. The rest is just bits and pieces.'

Jasper chewed on her plait thoughtfully. 'Is that interview on the Net?'

I shrugged. 'I guess the fan club has it. But it's really old. It wouldn't help us find where she is now.'

'Maybe not. But let's have a look anyway.'

We accessed the fan club and got the newspaper clipping up on the screen. It was ancient — at least five years old. The headline said 'Local Schoolgirl Wins Talent Quest'. There was a photo of a young, shy-looking girl holding a trophy. 'Mandy Miami wants to be a star,' the report said. Well, she'd done that all right. The rest of the interview was just the usual old stuff — where she went to school, the music she liked, what her parents did.

'There's nothing here,' I said flatly. 'Come on. We may as well admit it — we're beaten.'

'Shut up for a minute,' said Jasper absent-mindedly. She was reading the old newspaper clipping for the millionth time. 'What does it mean when somebody's in the hospi . . . hosp-it-ality industry?'

I was feeling so bad, I couldn't care less. 'I suppose it means they run hospitals. Why?'

Jasper shook her head. 'I'm sure it means hotels and motels. You know, things for tourists. It says here that's what Mandy's parents do.'

'So?' I couldn't see what she was getting at.

Jasper stared at me thoughtfully. 'If you were a celebrity who lived overseas, where would you stay when you came to visit Australia? Forget about Mandy Miami . . . where would *you* stay?'

I thought. 'I dunno. Home, I s'pose.'

Jasper suddenly snapped into action. 'So would I. And I bet you fifty dollars, so would Mandy.' She grabbed me by the shoulder and shook me. 'Celebrities are just like everyone else. They have mums and dads, and sisters and brothers . . .'

She was right. Even if I was famous I wouldn't stay in a big hotel when I came to town. I'd stay with Mum and Dad, in my own room.

'So how do we find out where her parents are?'

Jasper tapped the screen. 'It says here they're in the hosp ... hospit ... oh, you know, they run a motel.'

Something clicked in my brain. A motel ... I thought of what the Joker had said. *'This is a chat room not a miracle motel. Maybe you should try there ...'*

I turned to Jasper, my heart thumping.

'You get the telephone book. I'll get the bus timetable. And ring Frankie. See if she's home yet.'

She looked at me, puzzled.

'We're going on a trip,' I said. 'The three of us. To the Miracle Motel.'

We trudged up the dirt road for what seemed like hours. And then we saw it — rising out of the dry, dusty countryside like a mirage. A giant pink and blue flashing neon sign that dwarfed everything else around it.

MIR_CL_ MOT_L, it said. I had a closer look. Three of the letters weren't working. In fact the sign looked pretty prehistoric. The motel itself was nothing special ... just a low, white building with lots of bright blue doors. Frankie aimed her camera and started snapping photos.

'Gee, it looks a bit crummy,' said Jasper doubtfully. 'Are you sure this is it?'

'Well, there's only one Miracle Motel in the whole state. This has to be it.' I checked the road map again. 'Looks like this used to be the main road through here until they put the highway through. I suppose that's why it's so deserted.'

We walked up to the office, our footsteps crunching loudly on the gravel, and pushed open the screen door.

There was a girl sitting behind the reception desk, tapping on a computer. She wore big glasses and a red baseball cap.

She looked up when the door squeaked and smiled. 'Can I help you?'

'Yes . . . um, I, ah . . .' I stammered. I took a deep breath and collected my thoughts. 'We're looking for someone and we were wondering if you could tell us if she's here . . .'

The girl took off her horn-rimmed spectacles and started cleaning them with a tissue.

'Well, that depends,' she said pleasantly.

I glanced nervously at Jasper. 'Depends on what?' I ventured.

The girl put her glasses back on and regarded me

seriously. There was something about her that seemed almost . . . familiar.

'On whether you've got a joke to tell me. To add to my collection.'

You could have heard a mosquito sneeze. Nobody said a word.

'Oh, come on,' laughed the girl merrily. 'Don't be shy. I'll start. What goes pedal, pedal, crash!'

'A dork on a bicycle,' I said faintly. 'That's my joke.'

The girl extended a dainty hand for me to shake. 'You're Hugo Lilley, aren't you?'

I looked closely at her. There was something about her eyes . . . the way they twinkled. I was sure I'd seen them before . . .

'Well, aren't you going to say something, dear boy?' the girl said playfully. 'I always thought you had such good manners . . .'

'The Joker,' I breathed. 'You're . . . *you* are the Joker.'

The girl's eyes twinkled. 'That's my handle, yes.'

She took off the baseball cap with a flourish. A mane of long dark hair tumbled to her waist. 'But you can call me Mandy.'

Chapter Ten

'**H**ey! How about this for a headline?' Toby beckoned us over.

'MANDY MIAMI SPEAKS — A WORLD EXCLUSIVE by Chief Reporter Hugo Lilley.'

'Hmm ... I like it,' I said. 'Except maybe my name should be just a teeny-weeny bit bigger.'

'What about my name?' asked Jasper jealously. 'I interviewed Mandy too.'

'I've made yours a separate story.' Toby called it up on the screen. 'See? I'm putting it in a box with its own headline.'

'WHY BEING FAMOUS SUCKS — SUPERSTAR TELLS by Celebrity Reporter Jasper Lilley.' Jasper read it out loud. 'Cool! Is it going on the front page too?'

'You bet. Along with the photo of Mandy with the three of you. I think Mandy's dad did quite a good job for an amateur photographer.'

It was lucky Mandy's dad could point a camera straight because there was no way Frankie was going to be left out of that photo. I'd already looked at it a hundred times but I checked the picture again — just to make sure it was real. Yep, it was there all right — solid proof that the newspaper kids had done what every other journalist had failed to do. Tracked down the most reclusive pop star on the planet, and interviewed her!

'I still can't believe it,' sighed Jasper. 'One of the most famous people in the world . . . so talented . . . so smart . . . and she's my friend!'

Toby and I looked at each other and rolled our eyes. For someone who supposedly loathed Mandy and her music, Jasper did a brilliant impression of being totally and instantly star-struck the minute she laid eyes on Mandy.

'Funny how people can change their minds.' I couldn't resist taking a dig at her. 'I seem to remember Dad saying something about that.'

Jasper tossed her plaits. 'And I said, it would take a miracle. Well, we got one, didn't we? We got the Miracle Motel!'

Toby looked up from Myron. 'Shhh! Don't talk so

loudly. Remember, we can never tell anyone where we found Mandy.'

That was part of the deal. Mandy had agreed to talk to us, on the condition we never reveal her secret hideaway — or her Internet identity. If we did that, it would ruin everything for her. You see, as Mandy told Jasper, the worst thing about being a star is that people won't leave you alone. They're always pointing and staring and asking for autographs. When you're a famous celebrity, you can't even go to the corner shop without being mobbed. That's why Mandy had so many disguises. I'd been tricked at the airport by one of her favourites — the old lady.

'When I put on a disguise I can slip out into the street and just be one of the crowd,' she told us, a little sadly. 'It's so nice to be normal and not get noticed. People think it would be fun to be famous but believe me, it's not!'

That was one of the reasons Mandy always stayed with her mum and dad at the Miracle Motel. She just put on a baseball cap and some glasses, and helped out on the front desk like she used to do before she was a famous pop star. When she wasn't using the computer to check people in, she surfed the Internet as the Joker. None of the motel guests suspected for a moment.

When I told Mandy that one of the big music magazines had offered a one thousand dollar reward to anyone who could find her, she groaned.

'Do me a favour, will you Hugo?' she asked. 'After *Street Wise* comes out, take the photograph to that magazine as proof, and get the thousand dollars from them. And then donate it to my favourite cause . . . the crew-cut Pygmies. It'll help save their forests.'

Boy, did Jasper's eyes pop when she heard that.

'You know about the crew-cut Pygmies?' she asked Mandy.

'Sure.' Mandy nodded enthusiastically. 'When I'm not on tour, I raise money for their forests through the Internet. And I get other musicians to help me out. Like Razor X . . . have you heard of her?'

Red's not the word for the colour Jasper turned. She was bright purple with embarrassment. All this time she'd thought that Mandy didn't care about anything except being a pop star!

Still, Jasper made up for her mistake. She made sure that her story included a bit about Mandy raising money to save the Pygmies' forests.

'You'll mention the Pygmies won't you, Jasper?' Mandy asked earnestly. 'As a special favour?' It was just as well Mandy didn't ask her to swing naked from the tree-tops, because at that stage I think Jasper would have done anything she said!

As for my story, it included everything you ever wanted to know about Mandy Miami. How she wrote most of her songs while she was soaking in the bath with her favourite tartan shower-cap on; her favourite hobby — collecting jokes and riddles from around the world; and how she wanted to come back and live in Australia on a farm, so her dog Beanie had plenty of space to run around. All sorts of other things — except, of course, where we found her. That was a secret I promised to carry with me to my grave. That, and one other. You see, Mandy had so much fun talking to us that she promised to keep in touch with us on the Internet. So she gave me — you guessed it — her private E-mail number.

I was so busy daydreaming that Toby had to shake me.

'Earth to Hugo! Come in Hugo!'

I blinked. 'Oh, sorry. Just drifted off for a minute.'

Toby grinned. 'Well, drift off home, Scoop. Right now, I have to help Dad get ready for dinner. I'd better make sure he doesn't put his shirt on back to front.'

That's right — I'd almost forgotten. Mr Trotter was cooking dinner for Ms Lefty tonight to prove he could look after Toby properly.

'What's he making?'

'Beef Stroganoff,' replied Toby. 'He made it seven times yesterday and another three times today. We went through about two cows getting it right.'

'Is it edible, though?' asked Jasper, concerned.

Toby wrinkled his nose. 'Put it this way . . . it'll do the job. If there's one thing my father knows how to cook now, it's Beef Stroganoff. But if Ms Lefty wants to come back tomorrow night for something different, we're in trouble!'

'Don't forget — not a word to Mum and Dad about Mandy,' I reminded Jasper as we walked in the front door. Until *Street Wise* came out the next day, we couldn't tell a soul in Blue Rock about our Mandy Miami scoop. Otherwise, one of the other papers might steal it — not to mention Howard Fitzherbert. There was no way Mandy would talk to Howard now, even if he did manage to find her . . . but I didn't want to take any chances.

'Huh, speak for yourself, Big Mouth,' sniffed Jasper. 'I'm the one who's good at secrets, remember?'

As we closed the door, I heard Mum and Dad laughing in the lounge room.

'Sounds like they've got visitors,' I said.

Mum popped her head into the hallway. 'Oh, here they are! Come on in, you two. There's someone here to meet you.'

We walked in, mystified. A tall man with a shock of red hair and a friendly, freckled face was standing there, smiling at us. I'd never seen him before in my life. So why was he here to see us?

'Hugo, Jasper, this is the new teacher. Mr Bishop. He's replacing Miss Finch.'

The tall man stepped forward and extended his hand. 'Nice to meet you, kids. I'm trying to get round to meet all my new students before school starts again.'

For once, Jasper seemed to have lost her tongue. 'M-M-M-*Mister* Bishop?' she stammered, shaking his hand. 'Mr *Lindsay Bishop*?'

'That's me,' he said with a laugh. 'At least it was the last time I checked my mail.'

I felt a giggle rising at the back of my throat. What a surprise! All this time we thought Lindsay Bishop was a woman.

Once I got over the shock, Mr Bishop seemed really nice. With a start, I realised he was going to be *my* teacher this year. Jasper had gone up to grade six.

'Mr Bishop's just come back from overseas,' Mum said. 'He's been teaching at a little village school in South America for the last two years. Blue Rock Primary is very lucky to have him.'

So that's why Jasper couldn't find any trace of him! He wasn't even in the country.

Jasper suddenly found her tongue again. 'Have you been around to see everyone, Mr Bishop?' she asked innocently.

The new teacher shook his head. 'I'm running out of time, unfortunately. And there are so many new students to meet.'

Jasper's eyes lit up. I saw the look on her face and groaned inwardly. Mr Bishop didn't know it but he was about to be sucked in, big time.

'Well, I may be able to help you.' She smiled sweetly at him. 'You may not have heard yet, Mr Bishop, but I'm quite a well-known reporter in this area. How about doing an interview with me for our newspaper? An exclusive, of course.'

'Hold page three!'

Jasper, Frankie and I rushed through the door of the Cave later that evening. Toby looked up, surprised.

'Miss Bishop is a man and he's given us an exclusive interview, and Frankie has a photo.' Jasper collapsed into the old couch, breathless. 'We have to get it into *Street Wise*.'

'Miss Bishop is really a man?' asked Toby, bewildered. 'That *is* a good story . . .'

'It's Mr Bishop,' I explained. 'We all just assumed Miss Finch's replacement would be a woman.'

A big grin spread across Toby's face. 'Well, that'll teach us. And it just so happens I have a hole left on page three. I was looking for something to put there . . . now we've got it.'

'The last piece of the jigsaw,' said Jasper triumphantly. Then her face fell. 'The only thing is, we still haven't found your dad a girlfriend. I was planning on Miss Bishop . . . I mean Mr Bishop . . . oh, you know what I mean!'

'Don't worry about it,' Toby said. He seemed very cheerful all of a sudden. 'Somehow, I think everything's going to be all right.'

I peered out of the window of the Cave. The light in the kitchen was still on, and I could hear faint sounds of talking and laughing. 'Is Ms Lefty *still* here?'

Toby turned back to the computer.

'I think Dad's making her some coffee,' he replied casually. 'He wanted to prove to Ms Lefty how well he boils water.'

Hmmm . . . I looked at Toby suspiciously. I could have sworn he was trying to hide a smile.

'Come on, let's get this story into Myron,' he said crisply, changing the subject. 'I want this issue out on the street tomorrow.'

'With our world exclusive Mandy Miami story!' I cheered.

'And my world exclusive Lindsay Bishop story!' added Jasper.

'There's no way Howard can outdo us now,' said Frankie. 'The only thing his paper will be good for is wrapping fish and chips!'

Now that we'd saved *Street Wise* from going under, there was only one thing left to do. I jumped in front of the computer and accessed the Internet.

'What are you doing?' asked Toby. 'We have to put in Jasper's story about the new teacher.'

'I know. But there's someone I have to thank.'

I zapped off an E-mail and waited. The reply came back almost immediately.

> Hey dude! Long time no see! I thought you were lost in cyberspace — ha! ha!

It was my old friend Papa Razzi. A long time ago — or at least it seemed that way — he'd done me a big favour. Whether he knew it or not, he had set me on the path that led me, finally, to Mandy Miami at the Miracle Motel. Back then, I was just a newbie who had nothing to trade. Now it was time to repay him — just like I promised.

> Hi Papa! No, not lost — just caught in the Web. Listen, are you still Mandy Miami's biggest fan?

> Whaddaya think, Smart Alec? Of course I'm still her biggest fan!'

I sat in front of Myron and collected my thoughts.

Well,

I took a deep breath and started writing.

> Have I got a story for you . . .